PRAISE FOR

"Nelle L'Amour has hit her stride with Lauren and Emma Chase. Blake Burns is one of my favorite book boyfriends of 2014."

—*Adriane Leigh, USA Today Bestselling Author of the Wild Series*

"Not only is Blakemeister back, but he's on fire!! ...I cannot believe how even more beyond uniquely quirky, smooth, and honestly in a class of its own L'Amour's writing style is."

—*A is For Alpha, B is for Books Blog*

"THAT MAN, so romantic, so sexy, so passionate...I think I'm addicted to him."
—*Rusty's Reading Room*

"Zinging one-liners, alpha male hotness, steamy scenes and devious bitches!"
—*Fairest of All Reviews*

"Nelle L'Amour's writing is the perfect mixture of sexy dialogue, relatable characters, and laugh out-loud moments. Get ready to fall in love with THAT MAN all over again."

—*Vanessa Booke, Bestselling Author of the Bound to You series*

"Holy Hell! The amazing sex Jen and Blake have is out of this world HOTT!... This is one story that will blow your mind."

—*Whispered Thoughts Book Blog*

"Nelle gives you a story worth talking about...A true test of what love can overcome...When you get to the end ..you will want more."

—*Love Between the Sheets*

"This installment of the series is just as well written as the first...Laugh out moments and more emotional."

—*My Book Filled Life*

"Nelle L'Amour has a unique writing style...she can make you laugh and cry at the same time describing the ins and outs of the wedding from Hell."

—*As You Like It Reviews*

"The THAT MAN series keeps getting better and better, funnier and sexier. Bravo, Nelle! No wonder this series is a runaway success!"

—*Arianne Richmonde, USA Today Bestselling Author of The Pearl trilogy*

BOOKS BY NELLE L'AMOUR

Seduced by the Park Avenue Billionaire
Strangers on a Train (Part 1)
Derailed (Part 2)
Final Destination (Part 3)
Seduced by the Park Avenue Billionaire (Box Set)

An Erotic Love Story
Undying Love (Book 1)

Gloria
Gloria's Secret (Book 1)
Gloria's Revenge (Book 2)
Gloria's Forever (Book 2.5)

That Man Series
THAT MAN 1
THAT MAN 2
THAT MAN 3
THAT MAN 4
THAT MAN 5

THAT MAN 4

THAT MAN ₄

NELLE L'AMOUR

That Man 4
Copyright © 2014 by Nelle L'Amour
Print Edition
All rights reserved worldwide
First Edition: October 2014

This is a work of fiction. Names, characters, places, and incidents are either the product of the author's imagination or used fictitiously. Any resemblance to events, locales, business establishments, or actual persons—living or dead—is purely coincidental.

No part of this book of this book can be reproduced in any media or uploaded to the Internet without the permission of the publisher. If you would like to use material from this book (other than for review purposes), prior written permission must be obtained by contacting the publisher at nellelamour@gmail.com.

Nelle L'Amour thanks you for your understanding and support. To join her mailing list for new releases, please sign up here:
http://eepurl.com/N3AXb

NICHOLS CANYON PRESS
Los Angeles, CA USA

THAT MAN 4
By Nelle L'Amour

Cover by Arijana Karcic, Cover It! Designs
Proofreading by Karen Lawson
Formatting by BB eBooks

To all my Belles who asked for more of Blake and his tiger.

This is for you.

THAT MAN 4

Prologue

Jennifer

Paris~Five months earlier

"That *eez* a wrap," shouted our wonderful French director, gurgling the "r" in "wrap" the way I now knew only the French did.

We had just finished production on the first telenovela I'd overseen for MY SIN-TV, the block of programming I'd developed around popular erotic romance novels. *Shades of Pearl,* based on Arianne Richmonde's bestselling series.

The international cast and crew broke out in cheers. Among them were the lovely and beautiful Cameron Diaz, who had played the title character—her first television role ever—and her breathtakingly handsome co-star, Gaspard Ulliel, the French heartthrob, who played her much younger lover, Alexandre. Whoo-hoos mingled with hugs and out of nowhere, bottles of bubbly champagne popped.

I'd invited the author to the final days of shooting. A stunning, statuesque blonde, who looked like she could have easily played the part of forty-year-old Pearl, she was ecstatic. She enthusiastically gave me one of those double-cheek kisses.

"Oh, Jennifer! It's brilliant. Do you think we can win an Emmy?" she asked in her British accent.

An Emmy? To be honest, I'd never thought about that. All I'd thought about was making the best possible show for my audience. I wanted our viewers to love every sinfully sexy and suspenseful minute of it.

I shrugged my shoulders. "I don't know," I replied, but the fantasy of winning one danced in my head.

With a flute of champagne in her hand, the long-limbed Arianne sauntered off to mingle with the cast and crew. Suddenly, I felt very alone. I missed *that* man I loved terribly—Blake Burns, the head of SIN-TV and my fiancé—and wished I could share this triumphant moment with him. Reaching into my purse, I pulled out my cell phone and speed-dialed his number. It was 4:00 p.m. The time difference between Paris and Los Angeles was nine hours. That meant it was seven o'clock in the morning in LA. Knowing his routine well, he should still be at home.

To my utter disappointment, the call went straight to his voice mail. I left him a message, telling him how well the final shoot went. And for him to call me. My final words: "Oh, Blake, I miss you so much. I can't wait to see you." I was flying home tomorrow.

The cast and crew began to dissipate from the set.

Later tonight, there was going to be a big wrap party. To celebrate the completion of production, Conquest Broadcasting, SIN-TV's parent company, had chartered several Bateaux Mouches to cruise around Paris and party. I'd looked forward to the event, but now, missing Blake so much, it just wasn't as exciting.

A chauffeur-driven Peugeot sedan took me back to my hotel. While the stars and director were staying at the Hotel George V where we'd shot some scenes, I was staying at the newly renovated Ritz. It was like out of a fairy tale with its sumptuous décor and impeccable service. I'd never stayed in such luxurious accommodations before. They were so beyond. But what made the hotel even more special for me was this is where Ernest Hemingway, one of my dad's literary heroes, had written his early books. To his delight, I'd e-mailed him a photo of me in The Hemingway Bar and photoshopped the legendary author into the picture.

Wearily, I inserted my key card into the door of my tenth floor suite. Blake had insisted on getting a suite for me, and though I'd protested, trying to save the company money, there was nothing I could do. Being engaged to the head of SIN-TV and the future chairman of Conquest Broadcasting, came with its perks. Most of which I didn't need.

Dropping my shoulder bag on the gilded entryway console, I traipsed to my spacious bedroom with its regal canopy bed and breathtaking view of Paris. My eyes grew wide. Smack in the middle of the thick, fluffy duvet were two exquisitely wrapped boxes... one small, the other large. I recognized the wrapping of the small box immediately. With its signature hot pink heart, it was, of course, from Gloria's Secret. Gloria Zander, the CEO of the renowned lingerie emporium, was sponsoring my block, and she had a popular store right here in Paris on the nearby Champs-Elysées. Though eager to open the big mysterious package, I reached for the smaller one and peeled open the envelope inserted under the bow. A note with handwriting I didn't recognize met my gaze.

Congratulations on your first production! Wear these tonight.

The gift must be from Gloria. How thoughtful of her! With eager fingers, I tore off the wrapping and lifted off the lid.

My breath hitched. Inside beneath layers of delicate pink tissue paper was a magnificent set of pearl white lace lingerie: a demi-cup bra, matching bikini, and a garter. Plus a pair of lace-trimmed sheer silk stockings labeled: Made in France. Little bows embellished with pearls accented the lingerie in all the right places. The undergarments were exquisite enough to wear on my wedding day. I glanced down at the big snowflake diamond ring on my left hand, always awed by its sparkle and size and the memory of that magical night when Blake had proposed to me only a month ago. To my overjoyed mother's chagrin, Blake and I had not yet set a date. We had too much on our plates when it came to work.

Spreading the beautiful lingerie on the bed, I reached for the big package. My fingers anxiously unwrapped it. Inside the tissue-lined box was another envelope. I carefully slit it open with my index finger. Another note with the same unrecognizable handwriting. *And wear these too.* It must be another gift from the generous Gloria, I surmised as I unfolded the delicate paper.

With a gasp, I removed the contents from the large box. First, the strappy silver Jimmy Choos. And then the elegant ivory chiffon dress by my favorite designer and dear friend, Chaz Clearficld, from his new couture line, which Gloria had helped launch. It had a pearl-encrusted neckline, nipped waist, and full skirt. My size—a four. I'd never owned or worn a dress as stunning as this. Very grown up, it belonged on a movie star. Someone like Cameron Diaz. Or an elegant goddess like Gloria. Not a petite, middle-class, Midwestern girl like me.

I padded over to the imposing armoire and stood in

front of the mirrored doors, holding the dress up against me. Wow! I was going to look dazzling in it. And then my heart sunk a notch. If only Blake could be here to see me in it.

What a perfect night to cruise along the Seine. The mid May air was mild and the evening sky couldn't be clearer. Chartered buses had taken the *Pearl* cast and crew to the Pont D'Alma along the Rive Gauche from where the glass-enclosed boats were departing. Everyone was decked out to the nines for an evening of sightseeing, fine dining, and pure fun. Numerous partygoers, including Cameron and the very flirtatious Gaspard, came up to congratulate me on the production and commented on how *magnifique* I looked. I was both flattered and humbled. Paparazzi and publicists were snapping pictures at lightning speed. I smiled for the camera. But to be honest, while being Blake's fiancée and my career had launched me into this glitzy, star-studded world, I still wasn't used to so much attention and glamour.

On the quay, everyone was handed tickets, indicating which boat they would be on. I glanced down at mine. Number six . . . the last one. Carefully, in my new heels, I boarded the vessel and made my way to the upper deck. I leaned against the railing and took in the magical City of Light. The Seine quietly lapped against the side of the boat while my new dress billowed like a sail in the warm Spring breeze. The majestic Grand Palais faced me. All lit up, it resembled a giant jewelry box.

The rumble of motors of the other boats ahead of mine roared in my ears. They were taking off. I guess we were still waiting for more passengers to board this one because I was the sole person on it. Maybe there was another bus of people on the way?

Ten minutes passed. And still not another passenger. The other boats were now well on their way, and they began to fade in the distance. My heart began to race. Shit. Maybe, there was some kind of mistake, and I'd boarded the wrong boat.

"You look beautiful in that dress. Are you also wearing the lingerie I sent you?"

At the sound of that familiar sultry voice, my heart almost leapt into the Seine. I felt my insides melt. And my center grew as wet as the river itself.

I spun around. There he was. Leaning against the banister to the lower deck. *That man*. Who loved me body and soul. And mind. *That* devastating man. Blake Burns.

My mouth dropped. Speechless, I now understood why I hadn't been able to reach him earlier. He'd been flying. Flying to see *me*. And now, every part of me was flying because he was here.

Dressed in one of his impeccably tailored dark suits, he loped up to me. His long-legged gait was as sexy as his smoldering gaze. I sprinted up to him and met him halfway.

"Oh my God, Blake." My heart pounding, I flung my arms around him. "I can't believe—"

He tugged my head back by my ponytail, and then his mouth captured mine, cutting off my word supply. The tongue-driven kiss was fierce, passionate, and oh so delicious. With his hard body and colossal cock pressed against me, the boat began to move.

"Blake, where are we going?" I spluttered, finally breaking the kiss.

"The rest of the cast and crew are going on a tour of Paris. But you, my tiger, are going on a trip to the moon and stars and back."

"Oh," I squeaked.

He tweaked my nipples between his thumb and index fingers. I could feel them harden as he smiled smugly. Heat blossomed between my legs and then his hands slid down my hips.

He hiked up the skirt of my dress and shoved my soaked lace panties aside.

His fingers quickly found something delicate and responsive. My clit.

They circled it. Hard, just the way I loved it. Moaning, I rocked into him as his deft fingers picked up speed.

"Je vais baiser votre cerveau," he whispered in my ear, his accent perfect.

"Parlez-vous français?" I murmured back as a mind-blowing orgasm took hold of me.

"No, I talk dirty."

Blake

If you think I was going to let my little tiger party with that horny French frog, you sure as fuck don't know me by now. *Gaspard-Bastard.* When I'd awoken this morning at the crack of dawn, I'd hopped into the shower, thrown together an overnight case of bare necessities, and driven myself in my trusty high-speed Porsche to LAX. Jennifer had been in France overseeing her first production for over two weeks, and I missed her like crazy. And it wasn't just her tight little pussy I missed that my calloused fingers could attest to. I missed everything about her. Waking up to her in my arms. The taste of her kiss on my lips. Sharing showers. Her adorable giggle. And even the way she knew how to put me in my place. (Jeez. Another pun unintended?) Yes, my cock had a hearty appetite, but she'd shown me my heart hungered too.

Throughout the long eleven-hour flight, my cock had strained against my jeans while my heart beat like a jackhammer. I'd kept the tray table down the whole time except for the departure and landing. I couldn't wait to surprise her and see the expression on her pretty face. And then rid her of the lacy lingerie and that new dress, which I'd sent her with the conspiratorial help of Gloria Zander and her designer pal, Chaz. I was about to line up the three cherries . . . the right idea, the right person and, with no hitches, the right time. A big win was in store.

Timing, I'd learned, was everything. Without it, everything could fall apart. Even the best laid plans—or plans to get laid. Luck had it the flight arrived early, and I was able to get to the Bateau Mouche with ease. Little did my tiger know, I'd chartered it out of my own pocket for my own personal use. It was going nowhere until I was on board. And neither was she.

I fucking wish I'd taken a photo of her face when she set eyes on me. Her emerald orbs lit up like two stars in the sky, and her mouth dropped to the deck in a perfect O. An O big enough to accommodate my big ole cock. Damn, she looked hot in that dress. Magically, the river breeze blew the skirt up above her thighs, exposing her frilly garter and stockings and the scrap of lace panties I'd asked her to wear. My rigid dick was itching to get inside them. But first things first. I needed her in my arms. And my mouth needed to consume hers. It felt like years. She melted into me like chocolate, and as my tongue danced with hers, I scrunched up her silky dress. My hand landed between her thighs. Expertly, I maneuvered my fingers under her little lacy panties and found my hidden treasure.

"Oh baby, you're so fucking hot and wet," I moaned into her mouth as I rubbed her nub.

Picking up my pace, I had her panting against me. So ready to come. "Oh God, Blake," she cried out and then she let go.

I felt her shudder around my fingers while she clung to my shoulders so she wouldn't fall down.

My cock was on fire. With my mouth locked back on hers, I walked her backward until she was leaning against the railing. Her harsh breathing mixed with the sound of the soft waves brushing against the boat. I hiked up her dress once more and cupped her sweet ass. And then in one swift move, I tore off her drenched panties and spread her legs.

"Blake, what are you doing?" Her eyes were wide.

Monsieur Dirty Talker wasn't done with her. Do you seriously think I flew half way around the world just to flick her clit? I gnawed at her slender neck and got right to it.

"I'm going to fuck my future wife's brains out."

"But Blake, people on shore will see us."

"Don't worry about it, baby. We're never going to see them again. And when they hear you roar, believe me, they'll wish they were us."

"But, don't you think we should enjoy the cruise?

And take in all the monuments?"

"Tiger, there's only one monument in Paris you need to take in and it's right here." I zipped down my fly and out popped my rod. Nine inches of pure pleasure. It deserved a five-star rating on Yelp.

I nudged it against her, and in a hot breath, it was deep inside her. Her muscles clenched around my length. I hissed. I'd almost forgotten how good her tight little pussy felt. On the next breath, I was pounding into her ruthlessly, every thrust taking her closer to the edge. I clamped my hands firmly on her waist so she wouldn't fall overboard. Fuck. That would be bad. Her moans mingled with my grunts as I pummeled her harder and faster. Her face contorted with tortured pleasure, and I kept my eyes open to enjoy the beautiful sight of her. The beauty of Notre Dame, as the boat swung around the Île de la Cité and passed by the famous landmark, paled next to that of *ma belle dame* in my face and in my arms.

"Eyes, tiger," I ordered. I wanted her to enjoy the spectacular view too. On my command, she snapped open her long-lashed lids, and I rewarded her with another all-consuming French kiss—*la pelle* or shovel as some called it in France. In the distance, I heard promenaders along the Seine cheering us on with wolf whistles and applause. *"Allez, allez! A votre santé!"* I waved to them.

"Have you missed me?" I panted out as my cock

hammered into her. *Missed this?*

"Oh yes. So much."

Ahead of us, the Eiffel Tower sparkled. At the rate we were moving, it would be at least half an hour until the boat passed it, and headed back to the quay. My own lit up tower of steel wasn't going to last much longer.

"Come with me, baby." An intense tingling sensation surged from my sac to the tip of my shaft. I swear, my cock was going to jump out of its skin.

She emitted a ferocious roar you could hear in LA, and then I cried out her name as my own powerful orgasm met her blissful wake.

"Oh, Blake," she murmured, her voice, a breathy whisper.

Spent, I nuzzled her neck. "Are you happy I came?" Man, what was with me and these double entendres?

She sunk her head against my chest. "So happy."

With my arms wrapped around her, we stayed in this resting position for several long minutes as we aptly neared the Arc de Triomphe. So maybe we'd missed some of the sites along the Seine, but it didn't matter. I tenderly kissed her silky flesh everywhere I could.

Piano music drifted into the night air. Cole Porter. "I Love Paris."

"... in the springtime," I sang softly against her ear. I'd arranged for a romantic champagne-filled dinner for the two of us on the dining deck below—complete with a pianist and songstress. They were going to perform songs from the play list of *Pearl* to which we'd slow dance. And later fuck some more—I was saving her sweet pussy for dessert.

She sighed dreamily, never lifting her head from my heart.

Yes, I loved Paris in the springtime. There was only one thing I loved more—Paris in the springtime with my tiger. My future wife. I held her tight.

"Oh, Blake, I could make love to you all night."

That was the plan.

Chapter 1

Jennifer

"Happy birthday, tiger."

Groggily, I peeled one eye open after the other. Blake had insisted I take the afternoon off to spend time with my parents. After a whirlwind tour of Hollywood, we were all tired, and I headed home after dropping them off at The Beverly Hills Hotel where they were staying, courtesy of Blake's family. Late afternoon sunlight was streaming into the bedroom where I'd taken a much-needed nap. Through my hazy vision, I could see Blake heading my way. He must have gotten home while I was sleeping. Bare-chested, he was wearing sweats, and his hands were behind his back. I could stare at that glorious chiseled chest all day.

I forced myself to sit up. "Blake, my birthday's not till Monday."

He smiled that cocky smile I loved so much. "Yeah, I know, but I wanted to give you something before our dinner tonight with our parents."

Mom and Dad had flown in for my twenty-fourth

birthday. They'd been here since Monday and we'd had a great time. It was their first trip to Los Angeles since I'd started working for Conquest Broadcasting in their adult entertainment division, SIN-TV. One of the highlights of their trip was coming to my office. My mother, God bless her, kept saying "very lovely" though I knew she was having a mini-coronary each time she passed by a full-frontal nudity poster of one of our pure-porn prime time shows. She was relieved to see that my new executive office was tastefully furnished. Both my parents admired *The Kiss,* the sensuous erotic painting on the wall, and I told them it was a gift from Blake. Having to work, I sent them on a tour of the studio and made sure they got to see some tapings of shows as well as meet a few stars. My mother was in heaven when her idol Denzel Washington gave her an autographed headshot.

Unfortunately for them, they couldn't be here on Monday, the actual day of my birthday, because Dad had to go back to Boise. Though now retired from academic life, the university was making him a Professor Emeritus on the same day. It was a noble achievement and I, like my mom, was so proud of him. Unfortunately for me, my crazy work schedule with a dozen erotic romance telenovelas at various stages of production, made it impossible for me to fly back home to share his special day. I was thrilled, however, that they'd decided to come to California to spend some time with me. Tonight, for the first time, they would be going to Blake's parents' house. His mother had insisted on having them over for their weekly Shabbat dinner. I was sure by the time it was over they'd both know a little Yiddish—well, at least one word. *Shmekel*—that and *shtupping*—thanks to Blake's oversexed eighty-six-year-old grandma. I was sure this dinner was going to be the other highlight of their trip—for better and for worse.

Catapulting me out my mental ramblings, Blake sat down on the edge of the bed we now shared and handed me a small box. It was shiny red with a small white stick-on bow. "This is for you, tiger. Open it."

My heartbeat sped up. Blake loved buying me presents, and they were always so creative and thoughtful. And sometimes a little naughty. Carefully, I lifted off the lid. Inside was another small box—this one velvet. Removing it, I snapped it open and gasped.

"Oh my God, Blake, they're exquisite," I exclaimed, unable to contain my excitement or tears of joy. Glittering before my eyes was a pair of magnificent earrings—two dangling pink tourmaline hearts, each set with diamonds. They matched the pink tourmaline necklace he'd given me last Christmas. Tourmaline was my birthstone.

Grinning cheek to cheek, Blake planted a kiss on my forehead. "Put them on tiger, and I want you to wear them tonight."

"Oh, Blake!" I gushed, smacking his lips with mine. "I love you so much."

"The same." He watched as I inserted the pierced earrings into my earlobes.

"How do you do that?"

I laughed lightly and then rubbed the dangling earrings between my fingers. "I want to see what they look like on me in a mirror." I made my first attempt to get out of bed, but Blake held me back by the matching necklace I rarely took off.

He smiled at me wickedly. "Not until I give you your other present."

I glanced down and instantly had an idea.

Chapter 2

Blake

Yup, I did have another present for my tiger. But let me tell you, it was hard hiding this one. No pun intended. The tent between my thighs was sizeable, and it was expanding by the second.

The gist of my present was not lost on Jen. She gazed down at my crotch and her brows lifted.

"Oh, and what might that be?" she asked wryly, as if she didn't know.

I shoved down my sweats. "This one." Before her stood my big cock, gift wrapped in a big red bow. I suppressed a moan. It was fucking killing me because I'd tied the stupid bow on earlier—just tight enough so it wouldn't fall off—and now my pecker had practically doubled in size. What the fuck had I been thinking? The bow was cutting off my circulation and giving me numb nuts.

Jennifer burst into laughter. She was laughing so hard she was crying. I swear, if she didn't take this fucking bow off soon, my dick was going to fall off and I'd be crying tears too.

"Blake, that's the funniest thing I've ever seen," she managed. She was practically howling. "It's like you're God's gift to women."

"Take the fucking bow off," I growled.

Still roaring with laughter, she scooted off the bed so she was standing before me. With her nimble fingers, she undid the bow and tossed it on the duvet. I huffed a sigh of relief. Woof. That felt better. My cock recovered quickly and was ready for action.

"Jen, babe, do you think you could show *Mr. Burns* a little love?" Jen didn't know I reverently called my cock by a proper name (my little secret—that and the fact I also talked to my cock), but she got the idea. My eyes stayed on her as she bent over and kissed the wide crown. I pressed firmly on her head, coaxing her to go down on me. I hissed as that warm wet mouth of hers slid down my shaft, her tongue sliding along the backside. So fucking good. After taking me to the hilt, she came back up, adding welcomed pressure. She knew how I liked it.

That's all I needed, though truthfully, I could never get enough head from her. I was sufficiently lubricated for the next part of this gift. Before she could go down on me again, I gripped her ponytail and yanked up her head. She let out a little yelp that made my cock flex.

"Are you ready for part two of this gift?"

She eyed me suspiciously. "And that would be—"

"The fun part. You get to ride me."

Jen's face lit up like a little kid about to go on one of those coin-operated mechanical horsey rides. Wasting no time, she tore off my boxers she had on and repositioned herself, straddling my lap, knees bent on the bed, with my cock impaled inside her. Gripping her hips, I bucked her hard as she rode me up and down. I hissed. Fuck, yeah! This was good. So fucking good for both of us. Holding on to my shoulders, she got to control the pace while I got to go as deep and as hard as I could. I repeatedly hit her G-spot with each powerful thrust. She shrieked with pleasure again and again.

I gazed at her heated face. Her head arched back, she looked so impassioned, and I was mesmerized by the way the dangling earrings I'd just given her shook and shimmered. Quivering as if they were having little orgasms of their own. I was tempted to nibble her lobes but worried in my state of lust I might bite off an earring and swallow it whole.

I gripped her hips tighter as she accelerated her pace. The friction and heat of her rubbing against my thick length felt so fucking amazing.

"Do you like your present?"

"Oh God, yes!" she panted out. "I'm so close to coming!"

"Good, baby," I groaned.

On the next deep thrust, she fell apart with a thunderous "yes" and I could feel her throbbing all around my pulsing cock. Her body shook as I grunted out my own explosive climax and met hers full on. Spent and sweaty, we collapsed onto each other, her arms wrapping around me. We stayed in that position for several sweet minutes as we rode our orgasms out.

Five minutes later, we were nestled side by side, her head resting on my chest. We had almost recovered. Now close to five, the sun had begun its disappearing act and cast a mellow amber glow.

Jen traced lazy, ticklish circles on my chest. "Baby, I'll never be able to top that birthday present."

I playfully flicked the tip of her cute upturned nose. "Don't worry, you will."

"Do you have something in mind?"

"Yeah, I do." I was turning the big three-O.

"How 'bout a hint?"

"I want to wake up to my wife."

I felt her jolt against me. "What are you saying, Blake?"

"What I'm saying is I want to marry you on the day before my birthday."

"December twentieth? Gosh, Blake. That's only two months away."

"Jen, we've been engaged for almost six months; it's time to set a date. My mother has been driving me crazy."

Jen giggled. "Mine too. I keep telling her we've just been too busy at work."

Which was true. Except I'd checked our calendars

and had come to the conclusion that Saturday, the twentieth would be a perfect time to get married. With Christmas around the corner, most of our SIN-TV productions would be shut down, and our offices would be closed until January third—giving us an opportunity to go on a two-week honeymoon. I explained all this to Jen. She agreed. It made total sense.

She rolled on top of me and gave me a hot spontaneous kiss. "Oh my God, Blake, we're really going to get married!" The excitement in her voice was contagious. I smashed my lips against hers. "Yes, you're going to become Mrs. Blake Burns, and tonight we're going to break the news to our parents."

"My mother is going to be so excited." Jen beamed. "She's been planning our wedding forever."

I didn't know if Jen could feel my heart skip a beat. I quietly gulped. And so had my mother. Instead of letting her know this, I urged her to take a shower with me and get ready for our dinner.

The future Mrs. Blake Burns had another surprise in store.

Chapter 3

Jennifer

"Oh, my good Lord, you have a health club in your house?" Dressed in a demure A-line navy dress and sensible shoes, my mother couldn't contain her astonishment. Her soft gray-blue eyes were as round as marbles. While my dad had chosen to forego the tour of the Bernstein's forty-room Beverly Hills mansion and spend time chatting with Blake and his dad, my mom had taken Blake's mother, Helen, up on her offer. I'd accompanied them.

I didn't know whether to laugh or cringe. Neither my mother nor my father had ever set foot in a house of this magnitude and grandeur. One could easily confuse it with a five-star hotel with its size, amenities, and sumptuous furnishings.

I corrected my mother. "Mom, it's their in-home gym." But the truth, it looked more like a health club, the expansive mirrored room filled with racks of weights and a myriad of state-of-the art workout equipment. There was even an adjacent sauna, massage room, and steam room.

Helen twitched a small smile. She was elegantly dressed in a peach silk sheath and designer heels along with her usual array of mega-sized diamonds. Whippet-thin, the stunning woman, with her upswept platinum hair, towered over my lovely but humble Midwest mother.

"Saul and I work out here every morning with our personal trainers. You and Harold are more than welcome to join us tomorrow morning. And right afterward, our masseuse will be here."

Still in awe, my mother declined politely, letting Helen know that she and my dad would be flying back to Boise in the morning. The week had gone by so fast.

Helen glanced down at her diamond-studded watch. "Come, let's join the others for dinner. Everyone should be here by now."

The Bernsteins' weekly Shabbat dinner was about to begin. I couldn't wait to tell my parents as well as Blake's that we'd finally decided on a wedding date. Having planned for my wedding since the day I was born, my mom was going to be over the moon.

Shabbat dinner at the Bernsteins' house always had a special meaning for me. It was where I got an eyeful of Blake's super-sized cock for the first time. I'd accidentally walked into an unlocked bathroom where he was jerking off. I'd watched him come all over his hand. I was mortified, but now both Blake and I could laugh about it. The unforgettable memory, however, always made me very horny during Shabbat. And the same with Blake, though I wasn't sure if it was for the same reason. Always, in the middle of devouring Grandma's famous matzo soup, he'd reach for my hand, discreetly slip it under the table, and press it on the heated bulge between his legs. Tonight was no different. I could feel it throbbing. With my parents here, I wished for once he'd *"unbig"* himself to use the word he'd invented.

Most of usual suspects were gathered around the elegantly set dining room table—a dazzling spectacle of fine china, crystal, and silver. Joining Blake's parents . . . his feisty sex-crazed Grandma, who I adored, and his older sister, Marcy the gynecologist, who I hadn't gotten to know well. She and Blake were not particularly close. Missing, however, were her seven-year-old twin sons, who were home with strep, and Matt, her husband. Or rather ex-husband. Soon after Blake and I'd returned from France last Spring, a big family *scandale* had erupted. Marcy had discovered Matt, also a gyno, fucking one of their patients—a voluptuous blond starlet named Kristie who happened to be one of Blake's former hook-ups. Right in the Beverly Hills office the two of them shared. On the examining table, no less. Well, to make a long story short . . . Marcy got the practice, the house, and custody of the twins, and Matt got Kristie, whom he was planning on marrying. I'd wanted to reach out to Marcy—having gone through a not that dissimilar life-changing break-up with my ex-fiancé, Bradley. But the unspoken estrangement between Blake and his sister made it difficult. I did, however, admire the grace with which Marcy had handled her ex's affair. *The asshat!* And she now seemed more focused on her two children, who also seemed to be handling the break-up remarkably well. However, it did put a little damper on my happiness, and I sometimes felt bad when others in the family gloated over my engagement to Blake when her own marriage had gone down the drain.

As was customary in the Bernstein household, my mother, the female guest of honor, was asked by Blake's father to light the Shabbat candles. My darling Blake helped her do it. More memories of our first night together rushed into my head . . . his arms around fire-phobic me as I futilely lit one match after another. My mom got it on the first try and welcomed Shabbat into our lives. Shabbat, I had learned, was the symbolic union of man and woman, of God taking his bride. What a perfect time to announce our wedding date, though butterflies fluttered in my stomach. Setting a date made it so real. Blake and I were finally going to get married. I shot him a quick glance, soaking in his handsome profile. I could stare at him forever with that perfect outline of stubble and sexy mop of unkempt hair. He felt my eyes on him and shot back a flirtatious smile. The littlest smile could make desire pour through me like warm honey.

Over Blake's mother's delicious brisket, we made small talk, the Bernsteins mostly asking my parents about their stay in LA. Shortly, their housekeeper Rosa began to clear the table, making room for coffee and dessert.

"Oh, please let me help." My mother leapt out of her chair with her plate and my dad's along with their cutlery in her hands.

"Meg, darling," said Blake's mother coolly. "Please sit down. There's no need."

My mom shot me an awkward glance. I nodded, indicating for her to acquiesce. Rosa immediately took the plates and silverware from her, and my mother hesitantly sat down. Bewilderment flickered in her eyes.

God bless my mom. I loved her so much. She was such a good soul. Honestly, there wasn't a mean bone in her whole body. While Helen might chair lots of charities and foundations, my mother embodied charitable giving. Or should I say, living? She gave alms to the poor, never missed making meals for the homeless on holidays, and opened her door to anyone in need of a bed. Her whole life was about the needs of others, and foremost, those of my dad and mine.

Blake's father was grooming him to one day be the head of Conquest Broadcasting, and I'd have to adjust to that role. In my heart, I wanted to always be like my mom. Humble. Giving. Caring. And genuine. True to my roots. And one day, like her, I wanted to be a great mom.

Blake's grandma hurled me out of my thoughts. "So, *bubala*, *vhen* are you and my Blakela gonna get married?" Always the same question at around glass number three of wine.

I swallowed hard while Blake broke into his dazzling smile. Under the table, he squeezed my hand that was resting on his erection.

"Funny, you should ask, Grandma. Jennifer and I have exciting news."

My heart hammered. My mother's face was already lighting up. Blake continued.

"We've set a wedding date. Saturday, December twentieth."

A rapid-fire chain reaction was set off.

"Oy, I should only live so long!" moaned Blake's grandma, pouring glass number four. *"Zei gezunt."*

"Mazel tov," exclaimed Blake's father at the head of the table, raising his wine glass.

Blake's sister threw her arms up in the air. "Great. The same day as Matt's wedding to bubblehead. Now I have an excuse not to attend."

I didn't appreciate her mouthful of sarcasm, but she

was probably hurting. Blake shot her a dirty look.

My mother, oblivious to Marcy's off-color remark, had tears in her eyes. "Oh honey, that's wonderful. I'll call Father Murphy tomorrow to reserve the parish."

Helen's eyes grew as wide as they could. She'd definitely had one too many doses of Botox. Her harrumph silenced everyone.

"Meg, darling, there's no way we can have the wedding in Idaho. Or is it Iowa? I always get those two states mixed up. Regardless, at that time of year, the weather can be atrocious. I can't have our guests flying in those risky conditions."

Shit. I hadn't even thought of the weather factor when I'd agreed to Blake's date. But Helen was right. It could be blizzarding in the Midwest. With the airports shut down. And even the West Coast weather was volatile at that time of the year.

My stunned mother didn't blink an eye while Helen continued. "And as you can imagine, we have a plethora of guests to invite."

"How many?" ventured my father, showing no emotion.

"At least a thousand. Maybe more."

A thousand?

"I see." My pensive father pressed his lips thin while my poor mother gaped in shock. She seemed to be getting smaller and smaller in her chair. There was no way my parents could accommodate or afford a wedding of that magnitude. Why hadn't I thought things through? Her lifelong dream of making me a wedding had just left the planet. The look of defeat on her face was gutting me.

Finally, she built up the courage to say something. "Well, at least, Helen, let me help you plan it. I'm very handy, right Harold?" My mother, always looking for the good in the bad, turned to my father for moral support.

Helen responded before my father could say a word. "Puh-lease, Meg. Don't even think about it. With the wedding date so close, we can't afford any mistakes. Enid will handle everything."

"Enid?" I asked meekly.

"My mother's event planner," replied Blake flatly.

"Enid Shmeenid," chimed in tipsy Grandma. "Bubala, you and my Blakela should go to Vegas and elope."

"That's what Matt and I did," said Marcy, getting in her two cents.

Helen pursed her mouth; clearly, Marcy's elopement was a sore subject. She set her fierce gaze on Blake. "Blake, darling, we will have nothing of the sort. This is going to be the wedding of the century."

I hadn't even started to prep for the wedding and I was feeling all stressed out. My chest was tight. I met my mom's sunken eyes and then connected with my dad's. He wore a look of resignation.

Helen called out to the family housekeeper. "Rosa, please get me my phone."

Jumping at her beck and call, the uniformed Rubenesque woman scuttled out of the dining room and returned promptly with Helen's cell phone. Silently, she set it on the table and went back to cleaning up.

My eyes stayed on my future mother-in-law as she picked up the phone with her perfectly manicured hand and tapped the screen with a long red-lacquered nail. Putting it to her diamond-studded ear, she twitched a small smile, indicating her call had gone through.

"Enid, darling, Blake and his fiancée are getting married on December twentieth." She paused briefly, listening to the voice on the other end. "Yes, that would be wonderful if you could get the save the dates out this weekend. And yes, I'll get you the names of the McCoys' guests. I'm sure there won't be too many. And don't forget to book Rabbi Silverstein . . . and yes, that would be divine if you got the announcement into this Sunday's *New York Times*. MWAH, darling!" And with that, she ended the call.

My parents and I exchanged a nervous glance. I twisted my engagement ring. Reality set in like a crashing meteor. News flash: the wedding of the century had landed.

Chapter 4

Blake

After dropping her hushed parents off at The Beverly Hills Hotel, Jen and I drove back to my condo in tense silence. Following our announcement, the Jewish issue had come up again. Since we'd been engaged, we'd talked about it on and off, never coming to any resolution. Though they were secular Jews, both my parents wanted Jen to consider converting. For the sake of the children being their main bone of contention.

"Jewish *Shmewish*," my grandma had growled, with a dismissive flick of her wrists. "The only thing she needs to know is the *vay* to a Jewish man's *shmekel* is through his stomach. Learn how to be a good cook," she'd advised Jennifer.

Grandma's words had put a small smile on Jen's face. They had also turned it as red as beet soup. I loved my grandma, and you know what, she was right. Well, at least partially. Yes, I had a hearty appetite. But my cock had an appetite of its own, and my tiger knew damn well how to satisfy that. No one sucked me off better than Jen or could bring me to mind-blowing fulfillment while buried deep inside her ravenous pussy. She knew how to cook my cock to perfection.

I broke the silence. "Jen, we've gone over this. You don't have to convert if you don't want to. There's really no pressure."

She sucked in a short breath, a sexy sound that always turned me on. "It's not that, baby. It's the wedding."

"It's going to be spectacular."

"It's going to be a spectacle. And it's going to cost a fortune."

I made a sharp turn onto Wilshire Boulevard and picked up speed. I put the top of my Porsche up so we didn't have to shout above the whipping wind.

"Don't worry. My parents are going to pay for everything."

She turned to face me. Her eyes flared. "Blake, you don't understand. My parents were counting on making me a wedding. In their own backyard. Especially my mom. Didn't you see the expression on her face when your mother broke the news about that Enid lady?"

The truth, I wasn't really paying attention. While my mother's best friend Enid had planned all of my mother's philanthropic events and was indeed the most sought after party planner in town, I wasn't that keen on her planning something that was personally mine. Though she'd stayed close to my mother, she'd distanced herself from me. Our encounters were always cordial but cold. She carried a silent grudge. And time had not erased it.

I kept my feelings about Enid to myself. What Jennifer didn't know wouldn't hurt. I responded.

"Baby, *you* don't understand. My parents are like royalty in this town. They have a social obligation to put on a show and invite every Tom, Dick, and Harry they know."

"Well, your sister didn't have a big wedding." Her tone was confrontational.

"Marcy pissed my parents off. But she didn't care. I do. Part of my job is to make my parents look good."

Another thick wave of silence rolled over us as we neared my condo. Finally, as I pulled into the circular driveway of the majestic high-rise building, she cupped her slender fingers over my hand that was clutching the stick. I shifted into park and met her gaze. If anger had filled her eyes, it had dissipated.

"Baby, I'm sorry. I think maybe I overreacted. I've had this image in my mind of what my wedding would be like—it just wasn't a big flashy Hollywood one. But I get where you're coming from. And I don't want to let down your parents . . . or you."

Fuck, I loved her. And once we were upstairs in my apartment, I was going to show her just how much. The grateful kiss I smacked on her lips wasn't enough.

Chapter 5

Jennifer

After yummy morning sex with Blake, I rolled out of bed, took a shower, and got dressed. Jeans, sneakers, and my favorite USC sweatshirt. I was taking my parents to the airport.

"Jen, let me come with you. Or at least, let me get them a town car."

I gave my beautiful bedhead a peck on his forehead. "That's sweet of you, baby, but a limo is so not their style. Plus, I want to spend some time alone with them before they leave."

"Just be prepared to spend some time alone with me when you get back," Blake responded, ducking under the covers. "Quality time."

"Or do you mean quantity time?" I teased, his big dick filling my head. And in my mind's eye, my pussy too.

"Both," I heard him laugh as I waltzed out the door.

The Beverly Hills Hotel where Mom and Dad were staying was not far from Blake's condo. With no traffic on Wilshire, I got there in fifteen minutes. A feat by

Los Angeles standards. I didn't even have to valet my Kia. My punctual parents were already waiting for me at the curbside when I pulled up to the entrance. Amongst the throng of trendy guests dressed in the latest designer fashions, my parents, in their simple conservative attire, stood out like a sore thumb.

"Did you guys have breakfast?" I asked as I drove down Sunset.

"No, dear," said my mother. "I thought your dad and I could catch a bite at the airport."

With light traffic and time to kill, I decided to take my parents to The Farmer's Market on Fairfax. An old tourist attraction adjacent to The Grove shopping mall, it was a hubbub for tourists from Middle America. I thought after all the Bernsteins' fancy wining and dining they would like something down to earth. Something that reminded them of home. And reminded me of home. Old-fashioned DuPar's diner fit the bill.

We settled into a booth, me facing my parents. All of us ordered good old sunny side up eggs, hashbrowns, and bacon. Plus OJ and coffee.

"We had such a lovely stay here, darling," said my mother over coffee.

"The Bernsteins are fine people," added my father.

"Mom, are you really okay with Helen planning the entire wedding?" The crestfallen expression on her face when she heard the news was etched in my brain.

"Yes, darling. They have so many people to invite.

We could never accommodate them in our backyard. Nor could we afford the cost."

"But, Mom, Dad. You've wanted to make me a wedding your entire life."

"No, honey," said my father. "We've wanted only to make you happy our entire life. With the money we've saved for your wedding, we may do something else we've always wanted to do."

My eyes grew wide as did my mom's.

"What would that be, dear?" she asked.

"Sail to Europe on the Queen Mary."

My mother's eyes melted into my dad's. "Oh, Lordy! Could we really?"

"As soon as Jennifer and Blake tie the knot, I'm booking two first-class tickets."

Clapping her hand to her wide-open mouth, my mother let out a loud gasp.

I was brimming with happiness. My parents deserved this trip. In a way, Blake and his family were making it possible for them.

While I wanted to treat them to breakfast, my father reached for the check right away. It would be an insult to offer. My father was a *mensch* to use one of the Yiddish words I'd learned from Grandma. While waiting for the change (he had paid in cash), his eyes searched mine.

"Jennie, I want to ask you something."

"Shoot, Dad."

"Are you going to convert to Judaism?"

My mother looked at me unblinkingly; her faith and family traditions were so important to her. My stomach tightened. "I don't know. Right now, I can't fathom the idea of giving up Christmas and Easter."

My mother's expression relaxed as I continued. "Blake and I have discussed it. He's cool with that as long as we celebrate the Jewish holidays too and our kids have bar mitzvahs. I told him I want Father Murphy to officiate our wedding along with their rabbi."

My mother's eyes lit up. "That would be wonderful, darling. I think Father Murphy would really appreciate that. He's known you since you were a little girl and is such a close family friend."

My father nodded with approval. I was thrilled this decision pleased my parents so much. I made a mental note to discuss this with Enid, the wedding planner. But the discussion about Judaism wasn't over.

"Mom, Dad. I want to be honest with you. Down the line, I may decide to become Jewish. Would you be okay with that?"

My father smiled at me warmly and then clasped my hands in his. "Jennie, you must always know that both your mother and I are okay with *anything* that makes our little girl happy."

My mother grew tearful. "Honey, you're going to make a beautiful bride."

My father beamed. "And I'm going to walk my beauty down the aisle. *Zei gezunt!*"

I didn't know whether to laugh or cry. I did a little bit of both. How I loved my mom and dad! They were definitely the best parents in the world. And the most loving. Secretly, I made a wish hoping Blake and I would grow old together and have an everlasting love like theirs.

"Happy Birthday, darling," said my mother as my father placed a tip on the table.

"I'm sorry we can't spend it with you," said my father.

"Oh, Dad, it's your day too. I want Mom to film the ceremony and send it to me."

"Of course, darling," said my proud mother as she reached into the large tote bag parked between them. She handed me a package. "Your birthday present. I hope you like it."

I took the perfectly wrapped box from her and gently tore off the whimsical Happy Birthday paper. "Oh, Mom, it's beautiful! I love it!" Inside was a truly lovely ivory cashmere cardigan. I took it out of the box and brushed it against my cheek. "And it's so soft."

A radiant smile beamed on her face. "Oh, honey, I'm so happy you like it." With an equally radiant smile, I carefully folded the sweater and put it back in the box.

"And this is from me." Reaching into the tote, Dad

handed me a small package. From the looks of it, it was a book. Something he always gave me on my birthday. I eagerly unwrapped it. I couldn't help but smile. It was a Jewish bible.

"Read it, Jennie. It's not that different from ours."

Tears formed in the back of my eyes. I was going to miss them terribly after I dropped them off at LAX. But hopefully, the other Jewish education lesson I'd set up would keep my mind off them.

"Bubala, they're *gawgeous!*"

Blake's grandma wasn't talking about the gorgeous diamond and tourmaline earrings he'd given me nor about the gorgeous flowers I'd brought over.

She was talking about the matzo balls I'd just made. I poked my head into the aromatic, steamy kettle of soup simmering on her old fashioned Merritt and Keefe stove, and a big smile spread across my face. My matzo balls did look perfect—big and round—just like the ones Grandma made.

But, let me tell you, I didn't get them right the first time. Something went wrong and they fell apart the minute they hit the hot chicken broth. Honestly, they looked more like vomit bits floating around in a toilet. Yes, that bad.

The second time was hit and miss. A couple

worked; the rest fell apart or sunk. I was frustrated and deflated. Ready to give up.

Twice, we had to drain the broth, which earlier Grandma had shown me how to make. That part was simple. Just throw together some water, chicken parts (preferably kosher), celery, carrots, parsley, and a pinch of salt. Simmer for an hour and you couldn't go wrong. Matzo balls, however, could go wrong. Terribly wrong.

Grandma was so patient and the third time was a charm. I'd finally gotten them right. They were perfectly formed and fluffy. I'd lined up the three cherries—the right ingredients, the right consistency, the right timing.

"Trust me, Bubala, the way to a man's *shmekel* is his stomach. Blakala is going to go nuts over these."

I gave Grandma a big hug and couldn't wait to show off my new talent to my husband-to-be.

While the matzo balls cooked, Grandma and I retreated to the living room, the tantalizing aroma of the soup trailing us. After quietly asking her to show me how to make matzo balls at the end of last night's Shabbat dinner, she'd immediately invited me over to her guest quarters on the Bernsteins' property. Some guest quarters . . . her guesthouse was bigger than the biggest house in Boise. A mini-mansion. But unlike the Bernsteins' antique-filled palace, it was unpretentious and filled with cozy lived-in furniture and a lifetime of memorabilia. Tchotchkes and family photos were scattered everywhere. Many framed photos of a handsome man who looked a lot like Blake filled the room, including several with Blake as a toddler. And there was even an elaborately framed sepia photo of a beautiful young bride and her dashing husband on one of the walls. I studied it. It was definitely taken in the fifties. The stunning dress was Grace Kelly-like, but what most caught my eye, was the delicate lace veil that puddled all around her. It was a work of art.

"Is that you and your husband?" I asked Grandma.

Her face lit up. "Yes, that's my Leonard. The love of my life."

I didn't know much about Blake's grandma and felt a window of opportunity shining in my face.

"How long were you married?"

"Sixty-two years." Her wistful voice tugged at my heartstrings.

"How did he die?" I ventured.

"Do you really *vant* to know? Five years ago. One thrust and bada bing! I *vas* coming and he *vas* going!"

My eyes popped. Only Grandma!

She put a silencing finger to her mouth. "Don't tell *anyvon!* Our little secret. *Everyvon* thinks he died peacefully in his sleep."

Then, she clasped my hand. I promised I wouldn't say a *"vord."*

"*Oy*. Such a good man. A *mensch*. Her voice grew effusive. And oh *vhat* a *shmekel*. He *shtupped* me till the day he died." She paused and squeezed my hand. "Blakela reminds me so much of him. You've given me so much *nachas* marrying him. Such a *bashert."*

Before I could respond, the doorbell rang. The first member of Grandma's erotica book club filed in. Fifteen minutes later, they were all here. With their canes, dentures, reading glasses, and Kindles. One hour later, after a heated discussion of one of my favorite serials, Whitney G.'s *Reasonable Doubt*, which I hoped to option, I had no doubt. The book belonged on my schedule. And I had a lot to look forward to in my old age. A lot of laughs. Good friends. And gumming my hubby.

Chapter 6

Blake

I spent Sunday afternoon at Equinox where I played a mean game of racquetball with my best bud, Jaime Zander. I kicked his ass and hence he treated us to a round of beers at the upscale sports complex bar.

"We set a date for the wedding," I told him over a frothy Guinness on tap. "Saturday, December twentieth."

"Awesome, man. Where's it being held?"

"At my parents' house." I took a swig of the golden ale. "I think Jennifer was disappointed. She was hoping it would be at her parents' house."

"She'll get over it. It's going to be the wedding of the century."

I twisted my lips. "Yeah, that's what I'm afraid of. Anything my mother plans is always over the top and you can't get in her way."

"I hope I'm invited."

I smiled at my best friend. "You're more than invited. I want you to be my best man."

"Fuck, man. Get out. I'd love to. Come on, let's

toast." He lifted his mug and clinked it against mine. "To the wedding of the century."

"To making it through the wedding of the century."

We simultaneously took a slug of the beer.

Jaime set down his mug. "Let me give you a bachelor party."

"Let me think about it."

"Don't think too hard. It'll be fun. A guys' night out."

"What if you get me smashed and I go MIA?" I asked, thinking about the movie *The Hangover*. While every guy I knew found this flick hilarious, it creeped me out. I didn't want to miss my own wedding.

Jaime snorted and guzzled his beer. "Don't worry. I'll have your back. In the meantime, why don't you and Jen go out to dinner with Gloria and me tonight? Our treat. We'll celebrate."

"Thanks, but no thanks. It's been a crazy weekend. We're just going to hang out. Maybe order in and watch something on Netflix." *And fuck our brains out.*

"Sounds good, man," said Jaime, reaching for the check.

After showering, I headed home. I thought about ordering-in dinner while I was driving; I was that hungry. Maybe Thai or Chinese or something from that new Vietnamese restaurant that had opened on Westwood Boulevard. The thought of Jennifer and me feeding each other with chopsticks sent my cock into overdrive. I was hungering for her. A good game of racquetball often had that effect.

I opened the door to my condo and was greeted by a tantalizing familiar aroma. Upon hearing me enter, Jennifer came running out of the kitchen. Fuck. She looked delicious, wearing a dainty little apron over a pair of cropped leggings and barefooted.

She flung her arms around me and, on her tiptoes, gave me a kiss. "How was your game?" she breathed against my neck.

"Awesome. I creamed Jay-Z. And guess what, he's agreed to be our best man."

"That's wonderful. I'm going to ask Gloria to be one of my bridesmaids."

"Cool." With a sniff, I wrinkled my nose. "What smells so good?"

She smiled seductively. "I have a surprise for you." My eyes stayed on her as she dipped her hand into the deep pocket of the apron and pulled out a stunning jacquard tie.

"A new tie?" Jennifer loved to buy me ties.

"Mmm hmm," she purred. "I want to put it on you."

"But, baby, don't you think I should put on a dress shirt to get the full effect?"

"You don't need to right now." She stepped back up

on her tiptoes, and the next thing I knew, the tie was wrapped around my eyes like a blindfold.

"Are we going to have some kinky sex?"

"Maybe. But I've got another surprise for you." She took my hand and led me in the direction of the kitchen. The delicious aroma grew stronger.

"Sit on the counter," she ordered when we got there.

I hoisted myself onto the granite countertop. My imagination was flying. Was she going to suck me off?

"Open your mouth," she breathed.

I did as she asked, and on my next breath, a spoon with hot broth filled my mouth. I swallowed.

"Jeez, Jen. This is good. It tastes just like—"

"Your grandma's matzo ball soup. She taught me how to make it today."

"You spent the day with Grandma?"

"Yes. She's amazing."

I heard a spoon clink against a bowl.

"Okay, baby, now try one of my matzo balls." I felt her warm breath against my neck as she blew on the ball. The sexy sound and sensation made my cock twitch.

"Take a bite and tell me what you think."

My lips clamped down on the fluffy ball, and I bit into it.

"Wow! It's delicious. As good as Grandma's."

Still blindfolded, I could imagine my tiger's adorable smile as I swallowed.

"She taught me the trick to the balls. You have to use club soda."

"Soda *shmoda,*" I mock-mimicked Grandma. "Let me have another taste."

"My turn."

In my mind's eye, I could see her lips going down on the tender ball. Circling around it. Taking it into her mouth. My pulse sped up, and my own balls tightened as my cock strained against my jeans. What was it with matzo balls and Jen that turned me on every fucking time?

"Are there any other tricks to the balls?"

"Uh-huh. There's an art to rolling them."

Seriously? My cock was going stir crazy.

As if she read my mind, she yanked down my fly. Commando, Mr. Burns came flying out. She curled her fingers around my enormous erection, and getting down on her knees, began stroking it, hard just the way I liked it. Then, without stopping her hand action, she flicked her tongue along my smooth sack of balls, hitting a spot on the bottom that made me want to jump out of my skin. Holy shit! And if I wasn't already on my way to heaven, she wrapped her soft lips around them, rolling them around in her hot, hungry mouth, one big ball at a time. An insufferable electrical current spread from my head to my toes, the blindfold heightening every spark I was feeling. Squirming on the counter, I fisted her hair.

"Jesus, tiger," I hissed. "Is this what Grandma

taught you?"

"Mmm hmm," she moaned, feverishly sucking my balls and pumping my dick. It felt fan-fucking-tastic. She was making my soup to nuts fantasy a reality. Who cared if the soup was getting cold when my balls were on fire? An orgasm of titanic proportions was not far away. That telltale tingly feeling of fullness saturated my cock, and in a harsh breath, I came all over Jen's talented hand.

Back on her feet, she undid the tie. I blinked. My river of release was seeping through her fingers. She gazed at me, her green eyes glistening with pride. "Did you like that?"

Hell, yeah. I took her into my arms. "Is this going to be one of our rituals as husband and wife?"

She smiled sheepishly. "It could be."

"What other tricks did Grandma teach you?"

"What you can do with an apron is amazing."

Leave it to my sex-crazed grandma. I glanced down at the sexy little one strewn around her waist. "I'm eager to find out."

She cocked another smile. "Come on, let's finish the soup."

I jumped off the counter. "No offense, baby. Your soup is awesome, but I'm more interested in getting a taste of your new trick and anything else you've got cooking."

Her eyes smoldering, she draped her arms around

my shoulders. "Babykins, I've got a lot of things cooking."

"You're going to make one hell of a wife." I tore off her apron.

One breath later, we were fucking our brains out right on the kitchen floor. The strings of her apron bound around my wrists, I discovered what other wonders my bride-to-be had in store.

Chapter 7

Jennifer

"Happy Birthday, girlfriend!"

Libby was at the door of my office. Holding a small shopping bag, she barged in and placed the bag on my desk.

"This is for you. It's just a little something."

"Oh, Lib, you didn't have to get me anything," I protested, already dipping my hand into the bag. I broke into a smile. It was a T-shirt with "Mrs. Always Right" printed boldly on it.

"I know it's a little premature, but you need to remind 'Mr. Right' that you're the smart one."

"This is perfect. I love it." I stood up and rounded my desk to give my redheaded best friend a big hug.

"Why don't I take you out for lunch?" she asked.

"Can't," I sighed. I then explained to my future maid of honor that Blake and I had finally set a date and his mother was planning the entire wedding.

Libby knitted her brows. "Are you cool with that? What about your mom?"

"Yeah, we're both okay with it. With all the guests the Bernsteins have to invite, we don't have much of a choice." I glanced down at my watch. It was almost noon.

"Shit. I've got to go. Blake's mother set up my first meeting with the wedding planner."

I grabbed my purse and walked out of my office with Libby.

"Good luck. I want to hear everything. I can't wait to tell Chaz."

One for punctuality, I got to Enid Moore's office early. Located not far from Conquest Broadcasting's headquarters, it was housed in a lovely two-story brick townhouse right off fashionable Robertson Boulevard. Upon entering it, I was greeted by a stylishly dressed male receptionist, handsome enough to be called pretty.

"You must be Jennifer." His voice was effete yet warm.

I nodded. "Yes."

"Have a seat, sweetie. I'll let Enid know you're here. Can I get you some tea or water in the meantime?"

"I'm fine," I said, plunking down on the very formal loveseat and soaking in my surroundings.

The reception area was elegantly decorated in

shades of ivory, all silk and gilt, and lit by a crystal chandelier. Antique oil paintings of aristocratic brides were artfully scattered on the walls. Soft classical music piped through hidden speakers.

The coffee table in front of me was lined with impeccably arranged bridal magazines from around the world. In the center was a thick leather-bound album labeled "Moore is More." I lifted it into my lap and began flipping through the parchment leaves. Page after page was filled with photos of events that Enid had created. My eyes widened. Each event was more extravagant than the one before—ranging from a baseball-themed bar mitzvah featuring namesake baseballs at every seat and a life-sized ice sculpture of a young boy swinging a bat—oh my God, it was thirteen-year-old Blake!—to a Cinderella-themed wedding, complete with a pumpkin-shaped horse-driven carriage carrying the bride and groom and flower-entwined cages of white mice for centerpieces. I shivered, not knowing if the mice were real or not.

The sound of an intercom buzzed in my ear. I looked up from the album.

"Enid can see you now," said the receptionist. "Her office is upstairs." With a roll of his twinkly blue eyes, he wished me good luck.

I set the album back on the coffee table and clambered up the marble stairs. As I neared the last step, a shrill voice pierced the air.

"I personally don't care if you have to rent a private plane and go to France yourself. My client wants *fresh* mussels flown in from the Côte D'Azur. Period!"

Enid was still on her cell phone when I stepped into her office. She acknowledged me by lifting a perfectly manicured bony finger that silently said, "I'll be with you in a minute." Studying her spacious office, which was even more elegant than the reception area, I took a seat on a gold-leafed velvet armchair facing her desk. I kept my purse on my lap while she finished up her call.

"I will not take no as an answer. You're fired!" With a loud, exasperated huff, she terminated the call and slammed her phone onto her pristine desk, which looked to be a museum quality antique. My eyes stayed on her as she lifted, pinky finger out, a cup of tea.

For a woman likely in her fifties, she was extremely beautiful though surely preserved with the help of some nips and tucks and the magic of Botox. Her tight-skinned face with its high cheekbones and emerald eyes was made even more regal by her tightly pulled back jet-black hair. Substantial diamonds glittered on her earlobes, and a pair of pearl encrusted reading glasses dangled from a gilt chain and rested on her ivory silk blouse. She twitched a small smile. Something told me that was as far as her mouth ever went to avoid smile lines and other wrinkles. There was seriously not a line on her face.

"Sorry about that. A ridiculously impossible vendor.

Trust me, he won't be working in this town again." Her voice was now deep and breathy.

"No problem," I squeaked, admittedly intimidated by her.

"Well, let's get down to business. I'm extremely busy and am doing my dear friend Helen a big favor by squeezing you into my jam-packed schedule. Consider yourself lucky." She gave me the once-over. "I do hope you own a pair of contacts. Those hideous eyeglasses will never do on your wedding day."

"I do," I muttered, not happy with her insult. I liked my tortoiseshell glasses. They suited me.

"Good. One less thing to worry about. As you know, Helen wants her son's wedding to be the wedding of the century."

I nodded wordlessly.

She took a sip of her tea and then set the flowery bone china cup down. "I always thought my daughter would end up with Blake. Helen and I used to joke about it all the time."

A soupçon of suspicion niggled me. I wondered who her daughter was. My father's words of wisdom—curiosity killed the cat—stopped me from asking.

Enid sighed. "Bygones are bygones. Though you're not exactly in Blake's league—or my daughter's—I can't let my dear friend Helen down."

Internally, I cringed. How dare this haughty woman insult me like that? I had the burning urge to lash out at her and defend myself, but I bit down on my tongue. Starting things off badly wouldn't benefit anyone.

"Did Helen tell you anything about the way I work?"

"Not really." But I was already getting an idea.

"My motto, 'Moore is more' has made me the most sought after event planner in Los Angeles. In fact, the world. I just got back from Dubai where I created an *Arabian Nights* wedding for a young Saudi princess. At the reception, the bride and groom came flying in on a magic carpet. We're going to have to top that, aren't we?" She flashed that half-smile again.

Speechless, I nodded my head like one of those bobble head dolls. Gah! I just wanted something simple and elegant. I guess she never heard of the expression: Less is more.

"So tell me, do you have a favorite movie?"

What did that have to do with my wedding? I searched my mind. I loved animated movies and had several favorites, among them *Frozen*, *Despicable Me,* and *The Little Mermaid.* I randomly spewed the latter.

Enid's almond-shaped eyes lit up. "Fabulous. I love it. We have a theme."

"A theme?"

"Darling, all my events have themes. Yours will be an underwater fantasy. I can see it now. Guests will dance on a glass-topped aquarium filled with tropical fish of all sorts. You'll get married under a canopy encrusted with exotic seashells. We'll do a coral and white color scheme, and at the reception, we'll have stations of seafood flown in from all over the world—from fresh sushi made by the chef I work with in Japan to a boatful of shrimp straight from the Louisiana bayou. And of course, mounds of Beluga caviar from my preferred vendor in Russia."

As I listened, unable to get a word in, her voice grew more excited, and she began gesturing dramatically with her hands. "And pearls! What fun we can have with them! Hmm. Maybe pearl encrusted invitations. Ooh! Maybe we'll place them in giant iridescent plastic clamshells. With oyster white bows! A first! And of course, edible pearls all over the ocean-inspired wedding cake. And your dress. Don't even get me started on that. I'll have to call Monique right away."

"Monique?" I peeped. Talking about clams, I was clamming up.

Enid shot me a quizzical look. "Monique Hervé. She's one of my dearest friends as well as Helen's. Anyone who's anything in this town has a gown custom-designed by Monique. I'm sure you saw the one Star Davis was wearing at her nuptials, which, by the way, I coordinated. It was on the cover of *In Style*."

No, I didn't and I didn't care. There was only one person in the world that was designing my dress. "Excuse me, Enid, but I already have a designer in mind."

She looked taken aback. Unable to lift her brows or scowl, she pursed her fire-engine red lips. "Really? And who might that be?" Her voice was frosty. She obviously didn't like being challenged.

"Chaz Clearfield."

"Who the hell is he?"

"A young, up-and-coming designer. He's very talented and happens to be one of my best friends."

Enid's eyes bugged out. Suddenly, she reminded me of Cruella de Vil, and in fact, they could have been separated at birth.

"I. Don't. Think. So." Each word was a sharp staccato.

"What do you mean?"

"Monique is already committed. And the publicity this wedding will get will assure her hundreds of thousands of dollars in business. You should know she is a very big supporter of Helen's charities."

"But—"

Enid rudely cut me off. Her eyes flared. "Let's get something straight, Jennifer. I'm in charge here. Helen has put her trust in me to create a spectacular wedding. There are no buts. Are we clear on this?"

Shriveling in my chair, I nodded.

"Good. With the ridiculously tight time frame, there's absolutely no room for second guessing."

I twitched a nervous smile, acknowledging her. In the near distance, I heard footsteps—the clickety-clack of high heels on the hardwood floor in the hallway.

"My assistant should be here any second. With my hectic schedule, she will be your point person." She directed her gaze at the doorway. "And here she is."

I swiveled my head and my jaw crashed to the floor.

Enid's voice drifted into my ears. "This is my daughter, Katrina, who will be working with you."

Shooting eye daggers my way, Enid's daughter faced me.

Blake's ex hook-up.

Kitty Kat.

Chapter 8

Jennifer

I couldn't get my mouth to close. I was in a state of semi-shock. I just couldn't believe who was standing at the entrance to Enid's office. Kitty Kat. The catty bitch who had butted heads with me the night of Jaime Zander's art gallery gala and then kissed Blake at some black tie affair while we were broken up. The photo of her all over Blake had appeared in numerous magazines, including *The Hollywood Reporter.* If it hadn't been for Chaz, who'd been at the event and witnessed her aggressiveness, Blake and I might have never gotten back together.

Dressed to the nines in a body-hugging black mini-dress and six-inch stilettos, she was as stunning as ever. A tall, blond, D-cupped goddess who could have easily been a supermodel. The epitome of every woman Blake fucked until he met me. Her cat-green eyes, identical to her mother's, continued to clash with mine.

Enid's face lit up at the sight of her daughter. "Darling, don't just stand there. Do come in."

My gaze stayed glued on her as she slinked into her

mother's office. Her lustrous, shoulder-length tresses bounced like the hair you saw in one of those shampoo commercials. And her bountiful boobs bounced along in perfect rhythm. She held up her head proudly. Everything about her oozed confidence and sex. *And* trouble. My stomach twisted into a painful knot.

"Why, hello, Jennifer," she huffed, as she lowered herself into the armchair next to mine. Her cloying floral scent, the same as her mother's, assaulted me.

"Oh, I didn't know you two knew each other," chimed in Enid.

"Yes, Mommy. We met on one occasion."

One time too many, I thought to myself.

Enid continued while my blood curdled. Her words about a potential marriage between Blake and Katrina whirled around in my head. Did Blake have some kind of history with her?

Enid cut my disturbing thoughts short. "Since you'll be working so closely together, I thought it best you get to know each other. I've arranged a lunch for the two of you at The Ivy."

"And when would that be?" I asked, hoping the answer would be never.

"Why today, of course. With the wedding so close, we can't waste any time."

"But—" I had a boatload of work with deadlines.

Enid's eyes narrowed. "Jennifer, I thought we agreed. The word 'but' is no longer in your vocabulary.

We must work on a very strict schedule."

"Right."

I didn't know whom I despised more. And even worse, feared. Enid or her daughter.

The Ivy, the original outpost of the popular Santa Monica restaurant Blake and I frequented, was located on Robertson Boulevard, walking distance from Enid's office. Except I needed to drive. Not thinking our initial meeting would last long, I'd parked my car in a metered space with a thirty-minute time limit. There was an underground parking structure located just down the street and that's where I went. As I exited my car, a sharp pain stabbed at my gut. I winced. Just nerves, I told myself. The thought of having lunch with Kitty Kat was stressing me out.

I arrived at The Ivy before Kat and was shown to the umbrella-shaded patio table that had been reserved for us. As the waiter handed me a menu, I took in my surroundings. The place was bustling. Filled with slick Hollywood mover and shaker types, supermodels, and those philanthropic, fashionable ladies who lunched like Helen. I even spotted a couple of celebrities. I could handle coming to one of these Hollywood hot spots with Blake or Chaz, but by myself, I felt uncomfortable. Out of my league to use Enid's phrase.

My eyes darted to the street, and I saw Kitty Kat pulling up to the valet in her black Mercedes convertible. An attendant ran to open her car door and she gracefully stepped out of it. She kissed and made small talk with a couple of stylish women, who were waiting for their cars, and then loped up to the equally attractive hostess. They hugged. Obviously, she was a regular here. She spotted me and strode over to our table. All eyes turned to look at the long-legged beauty.

Taking a seat across from me, she set her monstrous designer bag on the brick patio floor and began, "I hope you know what you want because I don't have a lot of time. I have a mani-pedi I can't be late for."

The less time I spent with her the better. I immediately opened my menu and made a selection. A young waiter came by.

"Well, hello, Ms. Moore. Will you be having your regular?"

"Yes. A small plate of asparagus and a glass of champagne. The Perignon, please."

The waiter turned to me. "And you, madame?"

"I'll have the crab cakes and a passion fruit iced tea." Truthfully, I craved a glass of champagne to calm my nerves and numb my mind, but I didn't want to drink at lunch. I had a lot of scripts to get through today and needed to be clearheaded.

The waiter came back quickly with our drinks. Without any kind of toast, Kitty Kat raised her flute to her full glossy lips and took a sip. I latched on to my iced tea and curled my lips around the straw, taking sip after long sip so I didn't have to make any small talk with my companion.

Kitty Kat set down her champagne. "So, Jennifer, has Blake fucked you every which way?"

I gulped. The tea went down the wrong pipe, and I began to choke, spraying the amber liquid all over my silk blouse and the vintage floral tablecloth.

"Has he fucked your tits? He loves doing that."

I was coughing too hard to respond.

Her venomous eyes glared at my tea-stained chest. "I bet he hasn't. You're way too flat-chested."

My blood was bubbling with rage. I finally caught my breath. "Can we please talk about the wedding?"

It was as if she had deaf ears. Her eyes bore into me. "Did Blakey tell you we were an item?"

What?

"We both went to Buckley. He was crazy about me. Head over heels."

Wait! Blake didn't do love until he met me! "I don't believe you!" I snapped.

Kitty Kat smirked. "Oh, he never showed you any of our love letters?"

My heart skipped a beat and my chest tightened. I parted my lips, but words failed me.

"I'll take that as a no. So, I brought one along to show you." She lifted her purse onto the table and slipped a hand into it. A few rapid heartbeats later, she was holding a white manila envelope. My stomach churned as she pulled out the contents. A single piece of notebook paper.

"Take a look-see," she purred as she handed it to me. I instantly recognized the handwriting. The almost illegible scribble. Unmistakably Blake's. My heart clenched. And as I read the words of a poem, my hands trembled.

A million stars light up the sky;
One shines brighter I can't deny.
A love so special, a love so true;
A love that comes for very few.

At the bottom, it was signed in large block print letters: ITALY~BB

The letter slipped out of my shaking hands onto the table. I was having difficulty breathing. Finally, I managed a few words. My voice quivered. "It doesn't say anywhere that he loves you."

A poisonous smile slithered across Kitty Kat's face. "ITALY."

"That's a country," I countered defensively.

"Ooh. You're a smart one." Her voice was dripping with sarcasm. "And FYI, that's where we fucked for the first time when our families were vacationing together in Capri. We signed all our love letters that way. It's an acronym that stands for *I T*otally *A*lways *L*ove *Y*ou."

Tears were forming in my eyes, but I fought them back. *Don't let her get to you, McCoy.*

"Blake only loves me." My voice was desperate and watery when it should have been convincing and strong. I anxiously fiddled with my engagement ring.

A throwaway "ha" spilled from her lips. "He still loves me and I'm going to prove it to you. Besides, you're all wrong for him; he needs Hollywood royalty not some Middle America farm girl." She snorted like a pig. "He's just blindsided. You'll see."

Rage whipped through my veins like a rollercoaster. Impulsively, I grabbed my glass of iced tea, ready to toss it at her. However, my hand was shaking so vehemently the glass tumbled onto the table. The tea spilled everywhere, soaking Blake's poem. The words dissolved into an unreadable inky blur.

Kat's eyes flickered with fury. She screwed up her face, her lips snarling. "Look what you've done!"

"I-I'm sorry," I stuttered, springing to my feet. "I have to go."

Leaving Kat fuming, I skirted past the waiter, who was bringing what we'd ordered to our table, and sprinted down Robertson to my car. Tears were falling.

I desperately needed to talk to Blake.

Chapter 9

Jennifer

Blake was at his desk, his eyes glued to his computer, when I stormed into his office. His face looked intense.

"Blake!"

Upon hearing my voice, he looked up at me, startled as if I'd taken him out of deep thought.

"What's up?" He was being terse with me, something I'd never experienced.

"We need to talk," I replied, marching up to his desk.

"I can't right now. I'm in the middle of getting last minute P&L numbers together for my father's board meeting. He needs them by three o'clock to review. The meeting's at four."

"But it's important."

"This is more important. I can't be distracted. It's going to have to wait till later."

"When's later?" The testiness in my voice was thick.

"I don't know. The meeting could go late." He

paused. "Come over here. Let me give you a birthday kiss."

"I can't right now," I snipped, mimicking the tone of his earlier words.

"Fine." He stabbed the word at me and immediately returned his eyes to his computer screen.

Through pent-up tears, I stormed out of his office as fast as I had stormed in. So, work came first.

I spent the rest of the afternoon in my office, my door locked and my office phone set to "do not disturb." I pored over several scripts, in various stages of development, for the erotic romance block I'd developed for MY SIN-TV. I had a hard time concentrating. And I think I was being overly critical because I was in a bad mood. I'd desperately wanted to talk to Blake about Kat, but he was too busy. Okay. I got that, but it was the way he handled it.

After giving script notes, I watched a rough cut of an episode of *Shades of Pearl* based on Arianne Richmonde's popular trilogy. It was the sixth installment. Pearl (Cameron Diaz) was slow dancing with her now husband Alexandre (Gaspard Ulliel) in their suite at the Hotel George V. Goose bumps spread across my skin, and I was verging on tears. My viewers were going to love it. It was so sensual and romantic! I could feel what Pearl was feeling. The lust. The love. I'd gone to France last Spring to supervise the shoot. My first time in Paris. On my last day there, Blake had flown in and surprised me. And just like Alexandre, he'd taken me into his arms to dance and shown me that Paris was the City of Love. Our mind-blowing Bateau Mouche ride was just the beginning. Over the weekend, he'd fucked me senseless, sending me into outer space. There were not enough Michelin stars in the world to rate the delicious orgasms he'd given me. He knew every romantic hot spot in the city—from the most intimate restaurants to the expressive Wall of Love. A shudder ran through me. I now wondered—had he made love there with well-traveled Kat? I couldn't get her out of my mind.

Blake didn't bother to call or text me the rest of the afternoon. I guess he was still in the "very important" board meeting with his father. I glanced at my watch. It was after six. I decided to give his secretary, Mrs. Cho, a call to find out if she knew when the meeting would end.

"Me have no clue. Meeting go for very long time," she said in her charming Korean accent. "You want I tell Mr. Blake you call?"

"Don't bother," I told her. "I'll be heading out soon." We exchanged good-nights, and I hung up the phone.

My blood pressure was rising like bread in an oven.

I needed to talk to someone. Unload. Impulsively, I dialed Libby's extension. I inwardly sighed with relief when she picked up on the first ring.

"Jen. What's up? I'm about to leave."

"Do you have dinner plans?"

"I'm meeting Chaz for sushi at Roku. Isn't Blake taking you out for your birthday?"

"Can't. He's got a board meeting."

"That sucks. You can't be alone on your birthday. Have dinner with us."

Just the words I wanted to hear. And seeing Chaz would certainly cheer me up and set me straight with his brutally honest advice. "Really?" I responded.

Libby laughed. "Get over yourself."

I laughed back. The first time all day. I so loved Libby.

Roku was a popular Japanese restaurant located near the Beverly Center, not far from the house I used to share with Libby. Despite Don Springer's vicious sexual assault that almost cost me my life, Libby had chosen to stay when I moved out and moved in with Blake. She'd made the owner put metal grilles on the windows and added an alarm system for protection. She felt safe there and had turned my bedroom into an office.

Chaz ordered for all of us. Three large sakes and an assortment of delectable sushi, served in an extravagant bamboo boat. Libby and Chaz dug in voraciously with their chopsticks, consuming piece after piece of the artfully arranged rolls of raw fish. I picked at a California roll.

"You better have some more, Jen, before Chaz and I eat it all."

I took a sip of my hot sake. "I'm not that hungry."

"What's wrong, Jenny-Poo?" asked Chaz.

Guzzling the rest of my sake, I told Libby and Chaz about my meeting with Enid. And then about my lunch with Kat.

"She's just trying to intimidate you," said my analytical friend Libby.

"I'd like to slap the bitch," chimed in Chaz, who despised Enid's daughter.

"Why didn't Blake tell me about her?"

"You need to talk to him," quipped Libby, the researcher. "Find out what really went down between them."

"I tried to talk to him this afternoon, but he was too busy with last minute stuff for some board meeting. He practically ignored me."

"You can't blame him. The Conquest Broadcasting board meeting is super important."

Always rationale, Libby had a point. Maybe I overreacted. Yes, love was putting the needs of someone else before your own, but maybe that wasn't always possible.

I sighed and helped myself to more sushi. The hot sake was taking its effect, relaxing me a little. "How am I going to work with Kat?"

"You're not," chirped Libby.

"Easier said than done," I replied glumly. "It's not like I can tell her mother that. And I'm not comfortable getting Blake's mother involved. She and Enid are best friends. Enid handles all her events."

Chaz reached for another piece of sushi. "Wait till she sees you in the wedding gown I'm designing for you. It's going to be so faboo. The bitch will positively die over it."

My heart stuttered. I chewed down on my lip and swallowed hard. "Chaz, I've got some bad news." I paused, struggling to tell him the inevitable. "I won't be wearing your dress."

Libby's twin brother shot me a puzzled look. "What are you talking about?"

I felt tears clustering behind my eyes. "Enid has already commissioned some other designer. Monique Hervé." I didn't tell him how she'd dismissively blown him off.

"But, I've already started it. It's going to be everything you and I talked about and so much more."

Libby's eyes narrowed with rage. "Fire the bitch."

"I can't. Remember, I didn't hire her. Blake's

mother did. And to make matters more complicated, Monique is a big supporter of Helen's charities."

Libby folded her arms across her full-sized chest. "That sucks. But there's no fucking way I'm wearing anything else but one of Chaz's dresses. I'm not taking any orders from the Beverly Hills mafia."

Maybe Libby could be a rebel, but I couldn't. I met Chaz's chocolate gaze. "I'm so sorry, Chaz."

"Don't be, Jenny-Poo." His boyishly handsome face softened. "I'm going to make sure you get your dream dress regardless of whoever designs it. I'm going to be there every step of the way even if I have to smack one of those bitches till they get it right."

Libby slapped one chopstick against the other. "Smack the shit out of them, bro."

Oh, Chaz! Always there for me. Giggling, I felt so blessed to have him and Libby, my two best friends in the world, in my life.

We polished off the sushi (befitting given the theme of my wedding), and to my surprise, a small piece of complimentary birthday cake arrived at the table. After my two friends sang "Happy Birthday" at the top of their lungs and totally off key, I blew out the sparkling single candle and made a wish—I hoped my wedding would be perfect. And my dress too. Over the third large sake, we joked about the underwater theme of my wedding. Leave it to Chaz to make me laugh. We were pretty smashed and singing our version of "A Sailor Went to Sea, Sea, Sea"

"And all that he could see, see, see, was the bottom of Enid's ass, ass ass!"

Chapter 10
Blake

The board meeting was long and tried my patience. While my father, as always shined, I was distracted. I felt bad. I'd been short with Jennifer—on her birthday of all days. Maybe later, I could make it up to her. Lately, the pressures of work had interfered with our social life. My father was under a lot of pressure to live up to Wall Street's expectations for our fourth quarter earnings. The new Fall season had started out a little rough, but fortunately, Jennifer's block of programming was going through the roof. Daytime ratings for MY SIN-TV were the highest among all broadcasters, network and cable alike. The advertising dollars were pouring in, and we were seeing revenue from the joint online venture with Gloria's Secret. There was considerable talk in the meeting about spinning MY SIN-TV into its own 24/7 cable channel. I couldn't wait to share this news with Jennifer.

When the meeting finally broke at seven p.m., I immediately called Jennifer. No answer. Maybe she didn't have her cell phone with her or maybe she just wasn't answering. She was probably pissed at me. I was eager to get home, but my father insisted I join him and the board members for dinner at Maestro's, an expensive steak joint in Beverly Hills. He was the boss. I had no choice.

It was after ten o'clock when the dinner ended. I cruised down Wilshire Boulevard in my Porsche, the convertible down, keeping my eye out for a flower shop where I could stop and pick up a dozen fragrant pussy pink roses—Jen's favorite—along with a "Happy Birthday" SpongeBob balloon. Unfortunately, while I passed a few, not one was open.

When I got home, Jen was curled up on the couch, already in her SpongeBob PJs, reading a script. "How was the board meeting?" she asked without looking up at me or prefacing her question with a simple, endearing "hi."

"Long," I told her, trying not to react to the coldness in her voice. "I tried calling you, but you didn't pick up."

"I was in a noisy restaurant and had my phone on silent," she replied, her head still buried in her script though I didn't think she was actually reading it.

"I want to share some exciting news with you, but first I owe you an apology."

For the first time, she looked up at me. Her green eyes searched mine.

"I'm sorry I was so short with you this afternoon. I

was under a lot of pressure."

"Well, it seems like you can always find the time to fuck me over your desk, but when I have something important I need to share with you, you're always too busy."

Lately this was true. Work always seemed to come first.

I sat down next to her, my body brushing against hers. I nuzzled her neck. Instead of enjoying my company, she flung her script on the couch and jumped up.

"I'm going to sleep."

I leapt up from the couch and trailed her. "No you're not. Not until we talk."

"Leave me alone, Blake. I'm tired."

Fuck. I wasn't going to leave her alone. Catching up to her, I flipped her around and walked her backward until she was flat against the hallway wall. I held her pinned against it by her shoulders. The cherry vanilla scent of her freshly washed hair drifted up my nose. Almost a head shorter than me in her fuzzy slippers, she gazed up at me and shot lasers out of her eyes.

"Blake, why didn't you tell me?"

"Tell you what?"

"That you and Katrina Moore were a couple in high school."

"That's so fucking untrue. And what makes you say that?"

"She told me over lunch."

"Lunch?"

"Just for your information, she's going to be working with her mother planning our wedding."

"Shit." I let go of Jen's shoulders, but she didn't budge.

"She told me how she lost her virginity with you in Capri and how you wrote her love letters."

"What?"

"She even showed me one. It was a poem. I recognized your handwriting. I didn't know you wrote poetry."

My poetry skills were limited to dumb-ass limericks. I searched my memory.

"Jen, it was a twelfth grade homework assignment. We had to write a poem and then the teacher made us do an exchange. I got stuck with Kat. And I didn't write that poem. I copied a fucking Hallmark card. And FYI, I got a 'D.'"

My answer didn't seem to satisfy her. Distrust was written all over her pretty face.

"And what about Italy?"

"I was thinking maybe we'd honeymoon there," I said, glad she'd changed the subject.

Jen scowled. "I-T-A-L-Y as in *I T*otally *A*lways *L*ove *Y*ou."

"Tiger, I have no idea what you're talking about. I've never written that in my entire life. She must have imitated my handwriting and made that up. I swear, I'm telling you the truth. That girl is delusional. Yes, I did fuck her in Italy. It was a summer fling. And yes, I did screw around with her a little in high school."

I paused, the next words, ready to explode like a Molotov cocktail on my lips. I bit back my tongue.

"But nothing more. She's not even one of my hook-ups."

"Right." She stabbed the word at me. "You want me to believe that after I saw you together at Jaime's art gallery opening?"

"Jen, I was there alone. She happened to be there. She's a fucking stalker. She even followed me home that night. I swear, I almost had to call the police."

Jen's eyes stayed steady on my face as she digested my words. It was hard to read what was going through her head. I couldn't blame her for distrusting me with my checkered past. Her silence was killing me.

Finally, she parted her lips. "Why didn't you tell me about her?"

The softness in her voice and yearning in her eyes provoked me to run my hand along her jaw line. She didn't flinch. I looked deep into her soulful green orbs. "Because she means nothing to me, tiger. She's ancient history. I didn't want to upset you." *And I didn't want to go there.*

She fluttered her long-lashed eyelids. My cock tensed. I had to claim her. Let her know she was mine.

"There's only you, baby. I totally always love you. Only you. Every waking minute of the day. You do things to me no other woman ever has." I put her hand to my cock. It was hard as rock. And then I put her other hand to my heart. "My heart only beats for you. You own it. No girl has ever owned my heart except you. I want you to believe me."

"I do." Her voice was a whisper.

The sweet innocence of her voice aroused me. I pushed my hips against her, pressing my erection firmly against her center.

"You're the only one I want to fill. I want to fill your mouth. Fill your pussy. And fill your heart." Impulsively, I crushed my mouth against hers and gave her a fierce, passionate kiss as my hands slid down her pajama bottoms. I fiddled with my pants button and fly, and out sprang my cock ever so ready for her. With the help of my hand, I shoved it inside her, surprised she was so hot and wet. Placing my palms against the wall for support, I began thrusting into her forcefully, filling her to the hilt, while I tongue fucked her mouth and groped her tits. Groans escaped her throat and her breathing grew ragged. I picked up my pace, making my thrusts harder and faster. Her breaths came in pants and her groans became whimpers. She pressed hard against my shoulders, pushing me away and forcing me to free her mouth. Her face looked heated and impassioned. So fucking beautiful.

"Blake," she panted out. "Is this makeup sex?"

"If. You. Think. We. Had. A. fight," I grunted back with each successive, hard, long stroke.

"I'm not sure."

"Just shut up and let me fuck you." God. No one felt as good as my tiger.

"Okay," she groaned, letting me reclaim her mouth.

Without losing contact, I lifted her up against the wall. Wrapping her legs around me like a warm pretzel, she splayed her hands on my ass, and rocked her hips forward to meet my thrusts. Her whimpers morphed into shrieks, and I knew she was close to coming. Hard. I wanted to hear my tiger roar my name. So, I released her mouth again, not caring if she woke up the neighbors.

"Come for me, tiger," I urged, banging her into submission.

"Blake!" she cried out as she let go, her body shuddering inside and out with spasms of ecstasy. She clung to me as my own epic climax took hold of me, my load bathing her with sweet bliss.

Catching her breath, she rasped, "We should fight more often."

I smoothed her damp hair while she held on to me. "Nah, baby. We should just talk more often." And then I smacked my lips against hers so she couldn't say another word.

We fucked our brains out again and talked some more in my—I mean, *our* bedroom. Pillow talk was something new for me. Before Jen, I'd never spent the night with a woman. I had a rule. My hook-ups were plain and simple not allowed to share my bed.

The room was pitch black except for a sliver of moonlight that peeked between the curtains. We were spent and naked; while Jennifer was totally adorable in her SpongeBob pajamas or in a pair of my boxers, I'd take her in the buff any day of the week. She rested her head on my chest, my arm wrapping around her warm body. My fluffy duvet covered us midway.

She told me more about her meeting with Enid. Fortunately, Kat didn't come up again. The thought of her made me sick. She was trouble with a capital T, and I wasn't sure how far she'd go with Jen. I was going to have to deal with her and the past, but I wasn't sure how and when. Hopefully, she'd keep her fucking mouth shut. I forced myself to focus on what Jen was telling me.

"Are you shitting me? An underwater adventure?" Jokingly, I told her we could put SpongeBob blow-up dolls as centerpieces on all the tables.

She laughed. "I don't think so. Disney Ariel dolls are more like it. And she'll probably coordinate some kind of synchronized swimming production in your pool."

"Why didn't you tell her your favorite movie was *Jungle Book*, tiger? We could have had a zoo in our backyard, and you could have had Katy Perry show up and sing 'Roar' Or you could have sung it to me."

She playfully punched my chest. "Very funny."

I stroked her hair and got serious "Jen, you shouldn't have to be dealing with this bullshit." *And especially Kat.* "This wedding is stressful enough as it is."

She sighed. "I don't think I have a choice."

"I'm going to talk to my mother. It's your day. You should have the wedding you want."

While it was dark, I could feel Jen's eyes on me. "Blake, it's not my day. It's *our* day. We're in this together. I want to come with you to talk to your mother."

"Are you sure?"

"Yes, I'm sure."

"Okay, I'll try to set up something for tomorrow." Maybe the power of two would work. My mother was a force to be reckoned with, and Jen had only gotten a little taste.

I kissed my bride-to-be good-night and wished her a very happy birthday.

Chapter 11

Jennifer

Blake managed to set up a meeting with his mother on Monday at lunchtime. We left together from work and drove to Hillcrest, the exclusive country club the Bernstein family belonged to. Not far from Conquest Broadcasting, we drove into the gated property down a long tree-lined road to the entrance where a valet took Blake's Porche.

Although the Bernsteins had a tennis court on their property, Helen preferred to play tennis at the club where she socialized with her society friends. She had agreed to squeeze us in after her game. I'd learned from Blake that his mother had a very full life—every minute of the day was scheduled from the time she woke up to the time she put her sleeping mask back on. In addition to playing tennis and bridge, she chaired and sat on numerous cultural and philanthropic boards. The galas she organized were the talk of the town and raised hundreds of thousands of dollars for the charities they supported. Her other standing appointments included weekly visits to her hair stylist/colorist, manicurist, and facialist. She was so busy, Blake joked, that his father had to schedule sex with her. I believed him.

Helen was already seated at a linen-covered table when Blake and I, hand in hand, breezed into the club's busy, posh restaurant. Straight off the court, she was still in her tennis whites and wearing a visor. Her face brightened when she glimpsed us coming her way.

"Hi, Mom," said Blake, embracing her.

"Hello, darling. And hello, Jennifer," she added while Blake pulled out a chair for me. He then sat down next to me. A waiter came by with menus and told us about the specials. The poached salmon sounded good.

"I had a wonderful match with Lenore Waxman. I won both sets. Six-three."

"That's great, Mom," Blake said, studying the menu.

"She's so excited about the wedding. She even postponed her trip around the world to attend it."

Not wasting a second, Blake closed the menu. "Mom, Jen and I are having some issues with the wedding."

Helen's eyes grew wide. Like Enid, she couldn't lift or knit her eyebrows together. They probably went to the same skin doctor for Botox.

"I'm surprised to hear that. I just spoke to Enid who told me things are going swimmingly. No pun intended. The underwater theme is divine."

I built up the courage to open my mouth. "I mean,

it's very creative and everything, but I'd like something simpler and more understated."

Helen fluttered her eyelids as if she'd just heard her best friend had died.

Blake came to my rescue. "Mom, this is Jen's special day. She should have the wedding she wants."

"Blake, darling, it's a little too late. Jennifer should have spoken up."

Yeah, right. Dragon lady would have fried my ass.

Helen continued. "With the wedding less than two months away, Enid is moving at a very rapid pace. She's already started to design the invitations—the idea of encrusting them with pearls and delivering them in simulated seashells is positively divine—and she's ordered bolts of coral Thai silk for the tablecloths and tent draping from her vendor in Bangkok. And what do you think of this? She's lined up the U.S. Olympic Synchronized Swim Team to perform in our pool while our guests enjoy pre-wedding hors d'oeuvres and oyster shooters."

Blake and I shot each other an oh-my-God look. I was only kidding when I mentioned that possibility. A sinking feeling settled in. I was swimming up a stream without a paddle. No laughs. No pun intended.

Blake tried to reason with her again. "But Mom—"

I cut him off. It just wasn't worth it to create friction with his mother. I got it. Helen's way. Or no way. Things could get ugly quickly.

"Blake, we'll work with the theme. The wedding will be wonderful."

Helen flashed a smile. "Dear, it's going to be the wedding of the century. Generations will talk about it in years to come. I've lived for this day. My little boy's wedding."

Blake flushed while I forced a smile back at her. There was still one other big issue.

Blake read my mind. "We have one other issue."

"And that might be . . . ?"

"Kat." Just the mention of her name on his lips made my blood boil.

"What about her?"

"She's assisting her mother with the wedding plans. She's Jen's point person."

"Excellent. Enid could use some help. She's juggling so many events at once, including two I'm co-chairing in January."

Blake held his ground without getting into explicit details. "She's making Jennifer very uncomfortable. You know we have a history."

Helen flinched and then dismissively waved her bony, perfectly manicured hand. "Darling, let's not go there. That was ages ago. High school. I think it's wonderful she's following in her mother's footsteps. God knows, this town will need another Enid once she retires."

Our waiter returned to our table with a bucket of

champagne. He set down three fluted glasses and then poured some into each.

"Children, let's end this discussion and toast." She lifted her champagne glass. "To the wedding of the century."

Reluctantly, Blake and I raised our flutes and clinked them against hers.

Blake's mother had defeated us in our verbal tennis match.

"Well, that didn't go well," I said as Blake drove out of the club.

"It went well for my mother," he replied.

"Is she always like that?"

"Yes. Welcome to my world."

I'd spent some time with Blake's mother over the last few months at Shabbat dinners and a few events, but I actually hadn't gotten to know her.

"She's very set in her ways," Blake added.

"And your father puts up with her?"

"He more than puts up with her. He worships her. She's like a piece of jewelry. They have the perfect marriage."

"Elaborate," I said as we zipped down La Cienega. I wanted to know what he meant by the "perfect marriage."

"It's simple. Their roles are clearly designated. He's the king and the provider. She's the queen who makes him dazzle."

I deconstructed his words. What he said was true. I'd been to their home countless times and to several of Helen's events. She made everything beautiful. Including her husband. A shudder of self-doubt ran through me.

"Blake, I can't be that to you. I don't know how. Plus, I have a career I'm not giving up."

As we cruised down the busy thoroughfare, Blake was pensive. Finally, he responded. "Tiger, you're more to me than a piece of jewelry. *You're* my shining star."

I looked his way. Our eyes met briefly and then his returned to the road.

The words of his "poem" vaguely whirled around my head. "What do you mean?"

"You light up my life."

"I do?"

"Totally. You give me direction when I'm lost. You set me straight when I stray. And you take me places no one else can."

Tiger, tiger, burning bright. Oh, Blake!" His heartfelt words tugged at my heartstrings and sent a stream of tingles through me from my head to my toes. I had the burning urge to ask him to pull over and fuck him right in his car when I realized we had turned onto the

10 Freeway heading east.

"Blake, what's going on? Where are we going?"

"Vegas. My grandma was right. Let's elope."

Shock bolted through me like lightning. "Blake, that's crazy!"

"Jen, all I want is to marry you and for you to be happy. I don't need my mother's over-the-top wedding. I just need you."

My emotions swirling, I digested his words as he continued.

"We can get married at the Hard Rock. That place has meaning."

Indeed it did. It's where I totally fell in love with Blake Burns after a weekend of working, gambling, and dancing in his arms to Roberta Flack's "The First Time Ever I Saw Your Face." Every moment of that unforgettable weekend danced in my head.

"We'll get one of those Elvis impersonators to officiate," he said, cutting into my delicious memories and bringing me back to the moment. Reality set in.

"Blake, we can't do that. It would upset your mother and break my mother's heart as well as my dad's. My parents have lived to see me get married. And it would break *my* heart if they weren't at our wedding."

It was Blake's turn to think about my words. "I guess you're right," he mumbled, preparing to turn off the next exit.

As much as I loved him for caring so much about

my happiness, I was glad he hadn't lost his mind and pursued the Vegas idea. Eager to get back to the office, I got another surprise when he made an unexpected screeching turn into the parking lot of one of those roadside motels. The turn was so sharp my head swung out the window.

"Sheesh, Blake. You practically gave me whiplash."

"Sorry, baby. Between work and this wedding, I'm just really stressed out." He pulled the car into an available parking spot.

"Why are we stopping here?"

"Because there's a vacancy. And I need to de-stress and fuck your brains out. And fuck myself senseless."

Oh.

Chapter 12
Blake

Ten minutes later Jen and I were checked into Room 202. Trust me, with its cheap brown wood furniture, dingy floral bedspread and curtains, and worn out pea-green carpet, it was no suite at The Beverly Hills Hotel. But something about it made me fucking horny as hell.

I plopped down on the edge of the rickety wood-frame bed while wide-eyed Jen explored her surroundings. God, she was adorable.

"Blake, they have free SIN-TV here," she pointed out.

I wasn't going to need any porn. Just my tiger. "Baby, I want you to strip for me. Like a strip teaser."

Jen raised her brows and then quirked a sexy little smile. "Really? Are you going to compensate me?"

"Oh yeah, I'm going to compensate you big time."

"Some music would be good," she replied with a wink.

To get her in to the mood, I pulled out my phone and searched my iTunes app. "Bang Bang" fit the bill.

My tiger loved this song.

Strutting around the bed, she began to undress. My eyes stayed riveted on her slender figure as she slowly and sensuously unbuttoned her silk blouse, taunting and teasing me. The temperature in the room was rising by the minute. Hot damn. I loosened my tie and opened up my shirt. I was unwinding, but my dick was winding up. Way up.

"Bang, bang," Jen mouthed, her voice all breathy, as she sensuously slipped the blouse off her shoulders, whirled it around above her head, and tossed it to me. It was an easy catch. I kept it in my lap as I watched her massage her lace-encased pert breasts; her full lips parted in a sexy pout. God, she was good, totally getting into it. I knew from the day she stepped into my office and pretended to have a major orgasm there was more to this sweet little Midwestern girl than met the eyes. Yeah, I needed a good girl to blow my mind.

Thinking her bra would go next, she surprised me by taking off her pencil skirt, slipping it seductively down her hips. She gracefully stepped out if and stood before me in just her lace bra and panties and her heels. She splayed her fingers on her hips and gyrated. Bang, bang went my heart. Bang, bang went my cock. Mr. Burns was totally enjoying the show. Then she did something that totally drove my cock crazy. She pulled the elastic out of her hair and her perennial ponytail fell loose, her soft dark waves cascading over her shoulder like a sexy cape. She flung her head forward, her locks falling over her tits, and then flung it back, raking her fingers through her mane while she licked her upper lip with her talented tongue. Man, this show kept getting better and better. My cock was raging.

"Do you like what you've seen so far, Mr. Burns?" she purred.

"Come here, tiger," I growled, crooking my index finger. She sashayed up to me until she was standing between my spread legs. I dipped my hand into my pocket and pulled out a crisp one hundred dollar bill. I slipped the bill into her soaked panties, brushing my fingertips along her hot wet folds.

She shot me a satisfied, seductive smile and proceeded to expertly unhook her lacy bra. It slithered down her arms and, in the blink of an eye, it was sitting in my lap.

I studied her. Oh my sexy tiger—clad only in her scrap of lace panties and her heels. I inhaled. Mmmm. She already smelled of sex. So fucking intoxicating. On my next heated breath, I shoved her bikinis down and buried my face in her pussy.

I couldn't get enough of her. I licked, sucked, flicked, and circled. She tasted as good as she smelled. So sweet. So fucking sweet.

I planted my hands on her hips, and she gripped my shoulders as she let out moans. Rocking into me, she was enjoying every minute of this game as much as I was.

"Oh, Blake," she panted out. "You're going to make me come."

Not the time to stop my ministrations. That was the point. I wanted to give my tiger a mind-boggling orgasm and feel her pussy throb all around my tongue. I darted my tongue into her pussy while my right hand moved to her clit and took over.

"Oh God, Blake!" she shrieked.

Just hearing her say my name sent me orbiting. How the words of only one woman could send me flying into outer space. With a pinch of her clit, I sent her over the moon. As she came, she roared my name, and I looked up just in time to see the rapture on her face. Man, what a fucking beautiful sight!

Now it was my turn. Though she had barely recovered from her mega-orgasm, I flung her onto the bed. She was so spent she didn't resist. I frantically pulled down my pants and briefs and then mounted her. The bed made a strange creak.

Spreading her beneath me, I tore off her panties and plunged my hungry cock deep inside her entrance. Dripping wet, she didn't even yelp. I began to pound her. I mean *really* pound her.

Having one of those expensive memory foam mattresses at home, I wasn't prepared for this thrill ride. Man. Sex on this decrepit spring mattress was fucking unbelievable. The bounce was practically sending me flying, and I didn't have to work hard at pumping away. I don't know what was louder—the sound of our harsh pants, the rattling of the swaying bed, or the creaks of the ratty mattress. And I seriously wasn't sure which would last longer—the mattress or me.

Jen was thinking the same thing. Between pants of ecstasy, she breathed out, "Blake, I think we're going to break the bed."

Bang, bang. I didn't give a flying fuck. If the damn bed went down, we were going down with it. I picked up my pace, ramming ruthlessly into her at full throttle. What a cacophony of sounds—my body slamming against hers, our harsh breaths mingling with grunts and groans, and that damn boing-boing of the cheapo mattress springs.

And then one sound overtook them all. That of my tiger screaming to come. I moved my fingers to her clit, working it vigorously in circles the way she adored, and in a few breaths, she came with a roar. Craving my own release, I gave her one more forceful thrust, and as I exploded, the mattress crashed to the floor. Bang bang. Boing boing.

"Oh my God, Blake!" shouted stunned Jen as we went down.

"Fucking shit!" I growled, my cock still inside her.

Then we both burst out in hysterical laughter. I was laughing so hard it hurt, and Jen was practically in tears. After the stress of the last few days, laughing our asses off felt so fucking good. Still roaring with laughter, I cradled her head in my hands.

"Baby, we're going mattress shopping right after this."

"To replace this one?"

"No, baby, to buy us one just like it."

Chapter 13

Jennifer

Over the next few weeks, I learned that planning a wedding was a lot like producing a movie. It was a huge ordeal with much to commission, coordinate, and approve. Except unlike the erotic romance telenovelas I was overseeing, I was not the executive in charge of production. I would sum up the credits as follows:

Slate: Jen's Wannabe Wedding

Executive In Charge of Production: Enid Moore

Co-Producer: Helen Bernstein

Associate Producer: Katrina Moore

Gopher: Yours Truly

I was the bride. I was supposed to be the star *and* executive producer. The one in charge. Making the decisions. Selecting and approving invitations, flower arrangements, the menu, and lots more. Even being catered to. But this was hardly the case. I was more like a dispensable extra from Central Casting.

Because of the tight time frame, much of our correspondence and decision-making was done online. And it wasn't like I had a say. Whenever I got an e-mail from Enid regarding the wedding, it started off with two words "We have" As in . . .

We have created a Pinterest board to keep you abreast of our creative decisions. Please check it regularly. Today, I posted the most positively divine floral arrangement for the tables. A seascape of exotic flowers and seashells. Don't you just love the coral pedestal?

I must say, however, she worked at breakneck speed and was super organized. She'd created a To Do List and a timeline. Within one week, the following had been accomplished:

* A Save the Date had been sent to all twelve hundred potential guests via a Paperless Post custom design. Rather than a virtual envelope, a virtual scallop shell opened when you clicked on "You're Invited."

* A caterer was in place. Claim to fame: the coveted *Vanity Fair* Oscar party.

* A florist had been selected: "The Florist to the Stars."

* Extras had been hired to be part of my bridesmaid troupe. Per Enid, having only three—Blake's sister Marcy, Vera Nichols, and Gloria Zander—would look "positively pathetic" in publicity photos. I only hoped none of Blake's blond bimbos were among them.

* Photographers were in place. A dozen of them. Many would be shooting photos for various magazines, including *In Style*.

* A videographer was in place. Actually, it was the production team from one of Conquest Broadcasting's reality series.

* A twenty-piece band had been hired. But Enid was still hoping the Disney orchestra would come perform.

* Security was in place. There couldn't be enough. Paparazzi and wedding crashers were likely to abound at the Hollywood wedding of the century.

And that was just a partial listing. There was so much more to do—or should I say sign off on—including the final wedding invitation (to Enid's chagrin, the "right" pearls from her "preferred" supplier hadn't yet arrived), setting up a wedding registry, locking the menu, and putting together a play list. I wouldn't be surprised if Enid picked out all the gift items and decided what songs I should dance to with Blake and my father.

Last but not least, there was still the issue of my wedding dress. My dream dress. Or so I hoped it would be. Monique was out of town. I should have been thrilled at the prospect of meeting with her, but instead, the more time that passed by, the more I dreaded it.

My mom called me everyday to find out how things were going. So much of me wanted to unload on her. I missed her so much. I so wish she lived close by and could be here for me. I'm sure, if I asked, the Bernsteins with their billions would put her up (and my dad too) in a nano second, but that was so not my humble parents' style. Nor mine. Moreover, Enid, the shark, would likely eat my poor my mother alive. I assured her everything was going well. The truth: I felt overwhelmed and disconnected from my own wedding. The most important day of my life. To make matters worse, Blake had to embark on his yearly round of meetings with SIN-TV affiliates, which meant he was going to be out of town, traveling across the country for two weeks.

"Tiger, I'm going to miss you," he said on the morning of his whirlwind trip. Earlier, we'd fucked our brains out as if there were no tomorrow. "Are you going to be okay?"

I nodded. "The telenovelas are moving along great."

Standing at the doorway, his roll-away bag by his feet, he tilted up my chin with a thumb. "I mean about the wedding and everything."

I met his gaze. "Yes, baby, I'll be fine, but I'm going to miss you terribly."

"Same. I'll text you whenever I can and let's try to Skype every day. And you let me know if Enid or Kat cause you any problems."

The thought of sexting him every day and Skyping

him—and having virtual sex—cheered me up a little, but I knew the brunt of Enid and Kat was mine alone to bear while he was gone. Thank goodness, I hadn't had to deal with Kat since that horrific lunch, but who knew how long that would last. Standing on my tippy-toes, I kissed Blake for a long time, not wanting to let go of his kissable lips, and not wanting to say good-bye.

That morning I got into my office, feeling overwhelmed and downtrodden. I already missed Blake. I booted up my computer. My inbox was besieged with a barrage of e-mails from Enid, all *Subject: Wedding Detail*. One, in particular, marked URGENT, captured my attention and I opened it immediately. It was straight and to the point.

We have our first dress fitting today. Details below. It's imperative you be there. Be sure to bring a nude strapless bra and heels.
Where: L'Atelier de Monique Hervé
Address: 8420 Melrose Place, 2nd floor
Time: Noon

My stomach bunched up. With nerves, not excitement. What was wrong with me? I should have been excited about picking out my dream gown but strangely wasn't looking forward to it. Not one bit. And didn't Enid have any idea I had a high-powered job? She just assumed I could drop everything I was doing and race to meet her. Two words resounded in my head. *No buts.* I checked my Outlook Calendar, and luckily, my schedule was open at lunchtime, though I had no time to fetch the heels and bra. I immediately speed-dialed an important number. I wasn't going there alone.

I arrived at Monique's atelier early. Having boned up on my French in preparation for the *Pearl* telenovela, I know that atelier meant studio. It was located just above her eponymous boutique on chic Melrose Place—a short drive from Enid's office.

My eyes took in my surroundings. I felt like I was in some kind of fairy tale. Everything was white, gilt, and velvet with accents of girly hot pink. A regal crystal chandelier bathed everything in a warm glow, including breathtaking arrangements of fragrant white flowers on scattered pedestals. Above a glass console sat a huge, almost ceiling-high gold-leaf mirror, and in the corner, there was another massive tri-fold mirror. Bolts of tulle, lace, silk, and other fine fabrics were stored on built-in glass shelves, and elegant mannequins were clad in the most extravagant bridal dresses ever. There were also several racks of gowns gracing the marble floor.

A familiar breathy voice caught my attention. "Hello, dear." Theatrically stepping out from a pair of pink velvet curtains was Helen, wearing a stunning one-shoulder coral gown and flanked by Enid and Kat, dressed almost identically in designer black V-necked body-hugging silk dresses. My jaw dropped.

"Oh, Helen," I gushed with sincerity. "You look beautiful." She truly did, the magnificent silk-satin gown accentuating her svelte figure and the color complementing her platinum hair, cerulean blue eyes, and alabaster skin.

"Thank you, my dear," she beamed. "Monique is absolutely brilliant. She came up with the idea of the scalloped edges—so in tune with the theme of your wedding. By the way, Monique needs your mother's measurements. She has an equally wonderful idea for an oyster-white suit for the mother of the bride."

"Sure," I murmured, wondering how my mother would take this and wanting her to look as fabulous as Helen. I suddenly missed her. Terribly. Wishing she was here with me on the day of my first fitting.

An attractive petite brunette woman emerged from a back room. She was clad in a stunning chartreuse sleeveless sheath with matching heels. A tape measure was draped around her neck.

"Helen, darling, you must take a look-see in the mirror." I assumed she was Monique Hervé. I expected her to have some kind of foreign accent, but she didn't. She instead sounded very Valley.

Helen slinked over to the three-way mirror to admire herself. "Oh, Monique! It's positively divine."

Enid echoed the sentiment while Kat's poisonous eyes stayed focused on me. Monique turned her gaze to me and gave me the once-over. "So you must be the bride-to-be."

"Yes, I'm Jennifer."

She plastered a big fake smile on her face. "Wonderful. I have another very important client coming in shortly so let's get started."

"If you don't mind, I'm waiting for someone." *Where was he?*

Enid sneered at me. "Dear, we can't be wasting Monique's precious time. She squeezed you in today as a favor to me."

"Well, I guess I can start looking through the dresses on the racks." Having perused bridal magazines, I had in mind what I wanted—something with a vintage feel, either flapper-like from the twenties or Grace Kelly-like from the fifties.

Monique rolled her eyes. "Please, darling, there's no need. Enid and I have already chosen your dress."

I felt my blood bubbling. Didn't I—hello, the bride!—get a say?

My stormy eyes stayed fixed on Monique as she waltzed over to one of the racks and pulled out a gown. Folding it over her arm and not giving me the slightest chance to view it, she headed back my way and ushered me into the fitting room.

Fifteen minutes later, I shuffled out of the fitting room wearing "my" wedding dress and a pair of heels that were three sizes too big for me. Monique trailed behind me. Kat shot me a smirk.

"Take a look-see," trilled Monique.

I wobbled over to the tri-fold mirror. I glimpsed all three angles of my bridal self and not one put a smile on my face. My heart sunk.

"It's *magnifique!*" I heard Monique say.

Yes*, maybe* the dress was magnificent, but it was just not right for me. It was an extravagant shimmering white satin sheath that flared out in a cascade of ruffles below the knee. A mermaid-style dress, apropos to the wedding's under-the-sea theme. I could barely fill out the strapless top which was encrusted with crystal starfish, and what was supposed to be a body-hugging column hung loosely on my petite, boyishly narrow body. It was so baggy you couldn't even see my panty lines. The dress was definitely made for someone much taller and curvaceous. Someone like—

"Katrina, what do you think?" asked Enid, cutting my thoughts short.

She smirked again and snickered. "Personally, Mommy, I think it would look much better on me."

Her words stung me like a stingray but ran true. That's who this dress was made for. Blake's wannabe bride.

Enid absorbed her daughter's words and then turned

to Monique. "Monique, darling, it *is* a little big."

A little big? I was swimming in it. No pun intended.

Grabbing a heart-shaped pincushion from a nearby table, Monique asked me to step up onto a pedestal and began sizing the dress. "Don't move," she murmured, pinning the edges. My eyes stayed on my reflection in the three-way mirror. Even with all the nips and tucks (there were almost as many pins as there were crystals), the dress did nothing for me.

Monique admired her handiwork. "Much better. And we'll pad the top, maybe add a couple of spaghetti straps to hold it up, and sew in a butt pad to give you some curves."

"A butt pad?"

"Of course, darling. Everyone's wearing them ever since Pippa wore one to the royal wedding."

So I was going to be sitting on some kind of whoopee cushion at my wedding. My heart sank deeper as if an anchor was pulling it down. This was supposed to be one of the best days of my life, but it was so far from it. I felt like the Titanic.

Blake's mother glanced down at her gold and diamond beveled-faced watch. "Oh, dear, I'm going to have to say ta-ta. I have a board meeting downtown for the Philharmonic at one thirty." She scurried back into the dressing room and five minutes later, reappeared in her gazillion dollar designer pink silk suit.

She kissed me good-bye. "Darling, it's going to be

perfection. Sorry to have to go, but I'm leaving you in good hands." Hugging Enid and then Monique effusively, she asked them to send her a photo when all was said and done. In a breath, she was gone. I was shocked she wasn't staying for the entire fitting and more than ever wanted my mom to be here. Along with the other person I'd invited. Coming from downtown, maybe he was stuck in traffic. *Hurry!*

Monique made a few final nips and tucks. "You know, Jennifer, given how close your wedding is, you are *so* lucky this dress was available. I custom-designed it for a very famous rock star—whose name I can't divulge—but TMZ caught her equally famous fiancé in bed with an even more famous supermodel so she called the wedding off."

Great. So, I was going to be wearing someone's doomed hand-me-down.

"It would have taken months for the silk fabric to get here from Italy and forget about the genuine Swarovski crystals."

I gazed down at the glittery crystal starfish cupping my tits and hugging my hips, thanks to the pin-job. They did little to cheer me up. A welcomed familiar voice, however, did.

"Oh my frickin' God! That is so wrong!"

Chaz! Finally! Tearing my eyes away from the sad image in the mirror, I watched him storm into the atelier. His eyes clashed with Kat's. Poison daggers were going back and forth. Kat's lips snarled.

"What the hell is he doing here?" she snapped at me.

"I invited him. I wanted him here to give his opinion."

Chaz jumped back in. "Jenny-Poo, you look like Bridezilla! Take that hideous thing off immediately."

Monique's face darkened. "Excuse me? Did you just insult my one hundred thousand dollar creation?"

Gah! One hundred thousand dollars? Maybe some of the crystals were real diamonds.

Chaz held his own. "I don't care if it cost one dollar. A Las Vegas showgirl wouldn't be caught dead in that rag!"

God, I loved Chaz. He just told it like it is. He was so brutally . . . no, beautifully honest. He was right. Who was I kidding? The dress was *vomiticious.*

Flustered and obviously having a hot flash, Enid began to fan herself. "Jennifer, who is this intruder?" she panted.

Kat retorted before I could say a word. Her scrunched up expression was one of pure disgust. "Mommy, he's that man I told you about who called me rude at that Beverly Hills Hotel event back in January. The one Blake was at."

"Shut up, bitch!" Chaz barked. "Or I'm going to have to slap you."

All at once, Kat, Enid, and Monique gasped. I stifled a laugh.

Monique was the first to respond. "Whoever you are, I'd like you to please leave."

"My name is Chaz Clearfield, and I happen to be LA's hottest new designer and one of Jennifer's best friends. And she's going to wear *my* dress."

"Excuse me?" breathed Enid.

Kat turned to her mother. "Mommy, do you want me to call 911?"

My heart was in a flurry and my stomach twisted. A sharp pain stabbed me in the gut. Clutching my belly, I winced.

Chaz's eyes grew wide with alarm. "Are you okay, Jenny-Poo?"

I nodded, still in pain; I was sure, just stress. "Chaz, why don't I meet you at El Coyote. I'll be done here soon."

"Sure, honey." After a bear hug, he proudly sashayed out of the atelier, leaving me alone with the three barracudas.

Fifteen minutes later, the fitting was done and I was back in my work clothes. I grabbed my bag and headed to the stairs.

"Don't forget, Jennifer. Geary's at three o'clock sharp," Enid called out.

I stopped dead in my tracks and flipped around. "What do you mean?"

Enid scowled, making the tiniest crease in her Botoxed forehead, while Kat smirked. "Darling, don't tell me you've forgotten."

"I don't know what you're talking about."

"Didn't you read Katrina's e-mail? I've set up an appointment at Geary's to create your bridal registry."

"I never got it."

"Well, I sent it," snapped Kat in a snide singsong voice. "Maybe you need a new pair of eyeglasses."

Inside, I was fuming. She was lying. She *never* sent it. And probably deliberately.

"Where's it located?" I asked, trying hard to mask my anger.

Enid rolled her eyes in disgust. "Seriously, darling? It's on Rodeo Drive. I'm sure you'll find it. Helen is meeting us there, so please don't be late."

My eyes clashed with Kat's before I powered out the door.

"Oh God, Chaz. You're so lucky you missed the headpiece. It's some super-weird sequin headband concoction with this ugly rhinestone starfish that sits in the middle of my forehead." Another leftover from the rock star, who was obviously in love with being a star.

Seated in a booth at the popular Mexican restaurant El Coyote, I was on my second margarita and my thoughts were flowing freely. I dug into my tostada.

"Thank you, honey, for sparing me," replied Chaz, helping himself to another shot from the pitcher we'd ordered. He took a long sip and set his margarita glass on the table.

"Jenny-Poo. Listen to me. Go along with those bitches. I've moved forward on your dream dress and I'm not stopping."

My heart fluttered with happiness. "Oh, Chaz! Really?"

"Trust me, they're not going to stop you from wearing it on the day of your wedding."

Where there's a will, there's a way. Blake had ingrained these words in me. Chaz and I would make things work. Somehow. Someway.

A delicious lightness swept over me. I was going to be a beautiful bride after all. Wearing my dream dress. I couldn't wait to marry my Blake.

"When can I see it?"

"In a few weeks." As Chaz reached for the check, he looked at me sheepishly. "I have a big favor to ask."

"Anything."

"Would you find out if Jeffrey, Monique's receptionist, is single? He's so cute."

"Sure." A big smile lit my face while Chaz blushed. My father always said something good always comes out of the bad.

Geary's in Beverly Hills was glittering spectacle of china, crystal, and silver. It smelled of money. I was sent to the second floor where Enid, Katrina, and Helen were already gathered with a spindly silver-haired sales woman, who was holding an iPad. I recognized her. She was the woman who'd helped me at Bloomie's earlier in the year with picking out a gift for Gloria. And the woman who'd assisted my ex, Bradley, and his new fiancée, Candace, with their registry. She must have switched jobs.

"You're late," snapped Enid.

I glanced down at my watch. It was 3:05.

"We don't have all day so let's get started." She introduced me to the woman who would be working with us. Her name was Bea.

"Lovely to see you again," she said in her husky smoker's voice.

Enid looked puzzled. "Do you two know each other?"

"Yes, we met last year when I was still at Bloomingdale's"

"Such a despicable store," huffed Enid.

"Can I offer you ladies some champagne?" asked Bea, ignoring the putdown.

Everyone except me agreed to a glass. I still had a

buzz from the margaritas. Bea sauntered off, telling us to start earmarking items while she got the champagne.

"Shouldn't we wait to do this until Blake gets back in town?" I thought engaged couples were supposed to pick out their registry together.

Helen laughed lightly. "Puh-lease, darling. Men have no clue whatsoever when it comes to these kinds of things. You're so much better off he isn't here."

"And Blake obviously doesn't have a handle on the finer things in life," added Kat with a smirk. It was clearly an insult directed at me. It took all my effort to let it go.

"Jennifer, chop chop. Stop wasting precious time and get moving," urged Enid with a clap-clap of her bony hands. "I'm going to use the restroom and then I'll be right back." Helen and Kat joined her.

Truthfully, I didn't know where to begin. All around me were hundreds of dazzling china patterns, crystal glasses, and silver settings. Fit for royalty. Truthfully, I didn't want or need any of this stuff. Blake and I needed basics. Things like everyday china, dishwasher-safe silverware, pots and pans, and the like. Being a player and dining out most of his adult life, Blake had very few of these things, and we'd purchased just a few essentials when I'd moved in with him. I should be at Crate & Barrel. Not here.

I forced myself to meander through the store. My eyes bugged out. Everything was so super expensive.

Can you imagine—three hundred dollars for a teeny weenie eggcup? I mean, who in their right mind would gift such a thing? None of my friends or my parents' could afford even one. If they asked what to get us, I was just going to tell them whatever. Or to make a small donation to a charity in our names.

Examining a silver-rimmed dinner plate that at least reminded me of my mother's lovely Lenox china, I was distracted by a familiar voice.

"I should be registering, not you."

I spun around. Kat with a flute of champagne in her hand.

"What are you talking about?" My tone was sharp.

"Blake should be marrying me. I'm the one he really loves. You whored your way into his heart."

At her untrue words, a deluge of anger swept through me. "You're delusional. Blake even told me himself."

She narrowed her eyes at me. "Oh, and did he tell you about—"

"Darling." Kat's mother cut her off. "That's wonderful you're working with Jennifer. She can learn a lot from you."

She smirked again. "Yes, Mommy, she *can.*"

Enid sauntered off to join Helen and Bea.

Kat glowered at me. "Good luck, delusional one."

To my utter shock, she flung her glass of champagne at me and strutted off. My mouth hung open.

One soaked hour later, Blake and I had a registry that came close to $500,000. It included three sets of hand painted Limoges china (breakfast, lunch, and dinner), the finest Christophe cutlery, matching Baccarat wine and water goblets plus a set of flutes, a dozen Buccelati silver picture frames along with a complete tea service, and twenty-four of those little egg cups. Guilt rippled through me. Maybe after we were married, Blake and I could return all this shit. A half a million dollars would feed a lot of hungry children. And they sure didn't need eggs in eggcups.

Chapter 14

Blake

By the time I checked into my hotel, The Walden, where I always stayed in New York, it was going on eight o'clock. The rush hour traffic on the expressway from Kennedy into Manhattan had been nightmare. And made worse by some badass accident that every Tom, Dick, and Harry stopped to gawk at.

I plopped down on the king-sized bed, and propping myself against a mountain of fluffy pillows, I speed-dialed the top number on my contact list. That of my tiger. I hadn't even been away from her for twenty-four hours and I fucking missed her. She picked up on the first ring.

"Hi, baby. You landed okay?" She sounded tired.

"Yeah. I'm here. Are you okay?"

She launched into her afternoon. Shit. Fucking Kat was antagonizing her again. Every muscle in my body tensed. Sooner or later, the psycho bitch was going to let the cat out of the bag. While Jen went on about her disastrous dress fitting and the ridiculous wedding registry, I half-listened, debating whether I should tell her what had happened. Nah. It had to be done face to face, plus, I didn't want to ruin my little surprise. My cock jumped at the thought.

"Baby, I need you to do me a favor. Go to my office. And when you get there, lock the door."

A minute later, she was just where I wanted her. "Blake, what's this all about?"

"Open my top desk drawer. Inside you'll find a DVD. Insert it into my computer and watch it."

"Hold on." I heard the beginnings of a familiar theme song. I knew she was watching the DVD—various sexy poses of yours truly (including some photos from my modeling days) that I'd strung together with my own narration. Damn, I was good. Tom Cruise would be fooled.

"Good evening, Ms. McCoy. *That* man you're looking at is Blake Burns, one of this country's most dangerous sex addicts. Your mission, Jen, should you chose to accept it, is to capture Mr. Burns and make him come in his pants. As always, should you be caught in the act, my secretary will disavow any knowledge of your actions. This tape will self-destruct in five seconds. Good luck, Jen."

Jen's laughter mixed with the sound of a loud explosion. The DVD had faded to black, but Jen was still laughing.

"Are you kidding me, Blake?" she managed.

"Mission accepted?" I asked matter-of-factly.

"Accepted." Her voice was an octave lower and as sexy as sin.

"Excellent, Agent McCoy. You will need a special weapon to take him down." *After getting him up.* "Open the bottom drawer."

My cock already flexing, I waited impatiently as she did as I asked.

"Blake, a dildo?"

It was the biggest one I could find in the Gloria's Secret catalogue and even had one of those rabbit attachments.

"Suck on it."

Silence.

My cock rose another few inches. It was almost at full mast and as hard as rock.

"Lick it all over. Make it really wet. And don't forget to kiss those cute little bunny ears. For. Me."

While the line stayed quiet, I wished I'd Skyped with her. But as my father said, some things were best left to the imagination. Let me tell you, my mind's eye was getting a workout. A wild one.

"Now what, Blake?" Her voice was breathy.

With my boner straining against my fly, I shifted a little on the bed. "I want you to pull up that pretty little skirt of yours and bend over my desk. Click on your weapon and aim for your clit. Keep the phone on speaker nearby. I want to hear you loud and clear."

The buzz of the dildo sounded in my ear, but it was

soon washed out by her loud whimpers. I'd preset the vibration mode to extreme pulsation.

"Good job, baby. Now for phase two of your mission. Stick your weapon up your pussy."

"Okay," she breathed. I could hear her panting and imagine the glorious sheen on her face as well as her adorable ass up in the air.

"Oh my God" were the next words I heard. I could no longer keep my throbbing cock in my pants. With a hiss, I zipped down my fly and out popped my whopper. Holding the phone to my ear, I began to stroke it with my free hand to the beat of her desperate whimpers. I squeezed my eyes shut as my balls tightened, and the madness between my thighs intensified with each long, hard stroke. Close to the edge, I picked up my pace, stroking fast and furiously. My breathing grew ragged.

"Blake, I can't take this anymore," she moaned into the phone.

"Stay with me, baby. You're almost there." My hand galloped along my massive shaft as I imagined her soaked, throbbing pussy. My head arched back as my pulsing cock raced to climax. Oh sweet Jesus. Filling and swelling. On the next harsh breath, I exploded with an epic release that could make the Guinness Book of Records.

"Fuck," I muttered under my breath as a sweet cry of ecstasy sounded on the other end. I slowly peeled open my eyes and caught my breath.

"Tiger, are you there?"

Silence. Shit. Maybe she'd passed out. I imagined her collapsed over my desk.

"Tiger?"

"Blake." Her voice was just a tiny whisper. "That was amazing."

"Yeah, fucking amazing. You okay?"

"Yes. How did I do?"

"Baby, you can be on my team any day." I glanced down at my glistening semi-erection. *Mission accomplished.*

"I miss you, baby."

"The same." I crawled out of the bed, leaving my khakis behind though taking my phone with me. "I've got to wash up (oh boy, did I) and go out for dinner with my New York manager. I'll call you later. Where are you going to be?"

"I have my rape support group after work."

"Be careful. You know I don't like that neighborhood at night." I'd become as protective of her as I was possessive.

"Don't worry. I'll be fine. And then I'll be home dealing with wedding stuff."

At the word wedding, a chill skittered down my spine.

"Baby, if Kat harasses you, let me know. And don't believe a word she says. There's only you. Only you."

Chapter 15
Jennifer

I missed Blake terribly. He'd been away for over a week. Yes, he sexted and Skyped me, and we'd even had outrageous phone sex, but this didn't make up for not having him around. I missed falling asleep in his arms, and waking up on his chest, his heartbeat singing in my ears. And I missed seeing him at the office, sneaking kisses whenever we could. The touch and taste of his lips. Those kissable lips that had kissed me everywhere.

I was lonely. And a little on edge. Having Blake around made me feel safe and protected. The Springer incident had messed with my head. While we lived in a secure doorman building, an unexpected sound outside our apartment caused my heartbeat to accelerate, thinking someone might be trying to break in. And sometimes, I thought I was being followed, though when I glanced over my shoulder, no one was ever there. Other girls in my rape support group shared these insecurities. Dr. Williams, our group leader who had been a rape victim herself, said they were common.

Both Libby and Chaz were on the road—Chaz for trunk shows in major cities across the country and Libby for focus groups. Libby's findings along with ratings and quantitative survey research would determine which Conquest Broadcasting shows of the new Fall season would stay on the schedule and which would be canceled. I was thrilled my innovative block of women's erotic romance programming—MY SIN-TV—had tested through the roof. To my utter delight, Blake had told me there was talk of expanding the block and even creating a spin-off 24/7 women's erotica channel.

The only good thing about having Blake away was that I could focus on the wedding, especially at night. Every day after work, I came home to a boatload of gifts—so many that one of the building attendants had to pile them up on a dolly and cart them up to our apartment. Thank goodness, Blake had a spare bedroom. There was no place else to store all the boxes. It was almost filled to the hilt. The gifts came from all over the world, including a complete set of the eggcups from a Duchess in England who unfortunately couldn't attend the wedding. I'd become a master of writing thank you notes to people I didn't know.

E-mails from Enid besieged my inbox, and quite truthfully, I didn't have the time to open and respond to all of them during my busy work day. Everyday, she updated me on the RSVP list. The pearl encrusted invitations had finally gone out—yes, packed inside giant iridescent seashells, twelve hundred in all. The betrothal of Blake Adam Burns to Jennifer Leigh McCoy was now official.

We were already at six hundred twenty guests. The list was growing exponentially and that meant yet more gifts. More thank you notes. I seriously couldn't believe how many people the Bernsteins knew. Well-known television producers, directors, and stars were coming to the black tie affair from all over the world. And many politicians too. I perused the latest list. Oh my God. Even George Clooney and his new wife were coming. And so were Brangelina and the Clintons. I only hoped my mother could take a photo with Hilary.

Surveying the "C's" on the latest RSVP list, I spotted Libby Clearfield's name and wrinkled my brows. I'd invited both her and a guest—her longtime boyfriend Everett—but the response was not for "plus-one." Libby, my maid of honor, was intending to attend my wedding solo. I immediately speed-dialed her cell phone, having no idea where or what time zone she was in. She picked up on the second ring.

"Hi, Jen. I just got home. A quick break until I do my Midwest groups. What's up?" Her voice, so unlike her, sounded weary.

I got straight to the point. "Why aren't you coming to my wedding with Everett?"

Silence. A long, tense silence. Finally, my bestie

broke it. Her voice was small and shaky.

"Jen, I think I need to break up with him."

I reflected on her word choice . . . *need.*

"What do you mean?" Libby and Ev had been together forever, and despite the more than five thousand miles that separated them—she in LA and he in London on a Fulbright—neither had strayed from the other to the best of my knowledge. A moment of doubt hit me like a lightning bolt.

"Oh my God. Did Everett cheat on you?"

"Hardly," she said, her voice now tearful. In a heartbeat, she began to cry, sobs beating into my ear. Something so, so out of character for my sassy best friend. My heart was splintering.

"Lib, do you want to come over and talk?"

"I don't want to intrude on you and Blake." As close as we were, she was uncomfortable spending time in our condo. And because of the Springer shit that'd happened back in our little rented cottage, I was unable to go back there. Too many bad memories that ended in nightmares.

"Listen, Lib. Blake is out of town. Get your red curls over here, NOW."

She was on her way.

Libby looked tired. Her eyes were bloodshot—either from crying or the lack of sleep or both. The glut of focus groups, incessant travel, and whatever she was going through emotionally had taken a toll on her. Dressed casually in jeans and a USC sweatshirt, my curvy full-figured friend plopped down on one of Blake's oversized Italian leather armchairs while I went to the kitchen to fetch a bottle of white wine and a pair of goblets.

I curled up on the matching leather couch catty-corner to her and filled the glasses.

She took a couple of slugs and her freckled face brightened. "Wow, this is good stuff."

"Blake belongs to a wine club." I took a sip. "But to be honest, I kind of miss our Two Buck Chuck."

Libby smiled. "I'm still drinking it, but it's not the same without you."

I smiled back and then turned serious, ready for some answers. "Lib, what's going on with you and Everett? Why isn't he coming to the wedding?"

She exhaled. "It's complicated. I still love him, but it's not going to work out."

I knitted my brows. "What do you mean?"

"He wants to stay in Europe. He's been offered some associate professor position at a university in France. He's been pressuring me to quit my job and join him." She paused and took another sip of the wine. "Jen, I can't. My life is here."

"How long has this been going on?"

She ran her free hand through her flaming red mane. "A while."

"Why didn't you tell me?"

"With all that's going on with your job and the wedding, I just didn't want to bog you down with my mess of a life. We've been fighting a lot. In fact, we just had one tonight."

That explained the tears. Suddenly, I felt bad. Libby had always been there for me, but somehow I hadn't reciprocated. At least, recently. I mentally kicked myself.

"You should have told me. But I'm glad you're telling me now."

Setting her depleted glass on the coffee table, she reached for the bottle and took a glog straight from it. So Libby. So us. I grabbed the bottle from her and did the same.

"Maybe it would be good if Everett came to the wedding and you could talk things through." Poor Libby hadn't seen him for almost a year. Her joke that her vagina was going to shrivel if she didn't get laid was no joking matter.

Snatching the bottle from me, she shook her head. "I don't think so. The wedding will give him the wrong idea. And it would be very hard on me. I'm going to break up with him. I just don't know when, where, or how. I need to do it face to face. I owe him that."

Her hazel eyes grew watery. An unsettling thought entered my mind. "Lib, are you okay with me getting married?" I wondered if maybe she was jealous or threatened. Or just plain sad.

She set the bottle down. "Oh, Jen, of course I am. I'm so thrilled for you and Blake."

A bright smile lit my face. Despite initially not caring for my fiancé boss because she thought he was an arrogant, self-centered, egotistical jerk, which he sometimes still could be, my best friend had warmed up to him. Especially after he'd saved me from the monstrous Don Springer. A man who would slay for his woman scored big points in Libby's book.

"I'm so happy you're going to be my maid of honor," I said, the warmth of her words spreading through me.

Libby's lips flexed with a genuine smile. "Me too. I just wish I could be there for you more. This time of year is so busy for me. The focus groups won't let up until right before your wedding." She twirled a long, springy curl. "How's it going with Enid and the bitch?"

I caught her up on the dress situation and the latest developments. Her freckles practically jumped off her face.

"Oh my God! It sounds hideous. There's no way

I'm letting her turn me into some sleazy sea siren. Chaz is going to design my dress too."

"With your red hair, you'd make the perfect Ariel."

"No fucking way." She playfully threw a pillow at me.

"And listen to this, at each place setting, there's going to be a snow globe with a live tropical fish inside. The take-home party favor."

Libby made fish lips and held up the bottle. "To my best friend's wedding!"

It was time to uncork another.

Maybe Enid could dictate almost everything about my wedding from the invitations to the décor. But there were two things she wasn't going to have any control over: the dress I was going to wear and the person I was tossing my bouquet to.

In my heart, I wanted Libby to have her happily ever after just like me.

The next evening when I came home from work, I received the first wedding gift I wanted to keep. A splendid silver-plated, engraved wine cooler from Crate & Barrel and two cases of Two-Buck Chuck from Trader Joe's. A big smile warmed my lips as I read the enclosed note.

To My Bestest Friend in the World~

I can't wait to stand with you.
Cry with you.
Laugh with you.
And hold up Chaz's dress while you pee.

I love you so much~ xo Libby

Chapter 16

Blake

I used to love these two weeks of visiting affiliates. It was a glorified road trip—I flew first class, stayed in five-star hotels, and ate in the finest restaurants. I visited my stations, wined and dined my managers, and usually found some babe to fuck and forget. Just last year at this time, I was having the time of my life.

But all that was before Jen. I couldn't wait for this trip to be over. I got in and out of every city as fast as I could. Acting like an old fart. I visited each station, went out to dinner with the general manager, and then feigned fatigue so I could go back to my hotel room and catch up with my tiger. We sexted and Skyped, but nothing compared to having her in the flesh in my bed. Wanking off wasn't cutting it.

After a quick visit with my Sacramento affiliate, I'd flown to the East Coast and then worked my way back to LA. My last stop was Las Vegas. I was actually looking forward to being there. Not only because I was one stop away from seeing my tiger, but because I got to spend time with my favorite affiliate manager, Vera

Nichols.

Vegas was our top market, thanks to Vera. She ran her station with both an iron fist and a big heart. Her staff adored and revered her. And rightfully so. Her inspirational style of management was one for the books.

"You should have had Jennifer fly in," she told me over lunch at an Italian restaurant close to the station. "And by the way, Blake, her erotic romance block is killing it here. So many viewers have told us they want more."

I grinned. My tiger was brilliant. A star. And not just in bed. All across the country, I'd gotten the same reaction. A 24/7 erotica channel targeted at women was inevitable.

"I wish she could have, but she's so tied up with production. She's trying to get everything wrapped before our wedding."

"How's the wedding shaping up?"

I told her how my mother's event planner was putting it together at lightning speed and that it was going to be very over the top. I also told her about Kat's involvement.

"Geez, Blake. That must be awful for Jennifer to have to deal with her."

"It sucks for both of us." I wanted to tell Vera more. I knew I could trust her with my heart, but my father's words of wisdom resounded in my ears: "When in doubt, leave it out." I should have heeded them in the first place when it came to Kat.

Vera took a last sip of coffee. "I'm so honored Jennifer chose me to be one of her bridesmaids. I just need to figure out when I can fly into LA to be fitted for my dress."

"She's so honored you accepted. She thinks the world of you, Vera. Like I do." Vera was like a sister to me. And even more so than the one I actually had. I fought the urge to confide in her.

"Steve wants to take you out for drinks tonight," she said as I took care of the check. "He's going to call you later."

"Awesome." I looked forward to spending my final night in Vegas with Vera's husband. Tomorrow, I would be back in my office. First thing, I was going to have a closed door meeting with my Director of MY SIN-TV. I was going to fuck her over my desk.

I was staying at the Bellagio, one of the swankiest hotels in Vegas. While the Hard Rock was Conquest Broadcasting's preferred hotel, I made a point of not staying there because of the special memories it held for me. One day, Jen and I would go back there and fuck our brains out.

At nine p.m., Steve called me to let me know he

was here. When I got downstairs to the sprawling casino, not only was Steve waiting for me. Surprise. So was Jaime Zander. And an even bigger surprise—so was Jake, my roommate from college. The one who'd made me enter that crazy America's top model contest. Now that he was living in Silicon Valley, I hadn't seen him for over a year. He'd been through some bad shit but came out smelling like a rose. Something good had come out of the bad. Success agreed with him.

"You look fucking good, man," I said, giving him a man-hug. Along with Steve and some guys from the office, he was going to be one of my groomsmen.

"Where are we going?" I asked as the three of us, all casually dressed in jeans, headed toward the entrance to the bustling hotel.

I quickly learned we were going to have a guys' night out—a bachelor party so to speak.

"C'mon, man," said Steve as we filed into the Lip Service limo, courtesy of Jake, so we didn't have to think about drinking and driving. "You're going to sow your wild oats tonight."

"Don't lose me, dudes." Scenes from *The Hangover* flashed into my head. "I don't want to be hanging with any tigers." (Well, except the adorable one I was craving back home.)

The strip joint the guys took me to was off the beaten track. Despite being high-end, it was in a word—raunchy. All dark and smoky. Jaime had gotten us a reservation in the upstairs VIP room. The two of us nestled on the gaudy red velvet U-shaped couch while Steve and Jake plunked down on overstuffed club chairs. We shared two cylinder-shaped tables. A big tit cocktail waitress in a skimpy leather mini dress that barely covered her ass brought us a thousand dollar bottle of Cognac to go with our Cubans and filled our crystal snifters.

"To *that* man!" Jaime toasted, aiming his balloon glass at me. We clinked and chugged the shots.

As the velvety orange liquid warmed my blood, swirls of colorful disco lights bathed the scarlet walls and music piped through the speakers. Wouldn't you know it? "Bang Bang"—the very song Jen had stripped to a few weeks ago.

"Here comes your girl," sang Steve, refilling our glasses.

"Whoof!" mumbled Jake, blowing a ring of smoke.

Strutting my way was five feet ten inches of pure plastic. Bikini clad, tatted, and wearing tacky as shit platforms. I gulped my drink. Fuck. I recognized her. She was one of the blond bimbos who'd assaulted me at the Hard Rock pool and put a rift of misunderstanding between Jennifer and me. Jennifer's stinging words whirled around in my head. "No girl means anything to you." What a difference a year could make. And what a difference one special girl could make.

"Hiya, handsome," she cooed, hurling me into the

moment with a seductive come-on. "Nice seeing you again."

"You know each other?" laughed Jaime, sucking on his cigar.

"Oh yeah," said Kelly or Keely or whatever the fuck her name was. "But now we're going to get to know each other better."

Downing their cognacs, the boys roared as she straddled her long legs over my lap. She was in my face. Her musky scent nauseated me. She smelled nothing of cherries and vanilla.

She began to do her thing. Pouting. Licking her lips. Gyrating her hips. Grinding my thighs. Swinging her melon-sized tits. Brushing them against me. Flinging her brassy mane. Touching herself all over. Smashed, my buddies were getting off on her, howling, "Whoo hoo! Fuck! Go, baby!" If only Gloria and Vera could see them.

You'd think my cock would be in overdrive. Bang bang. Don't let my genitals fool you. Forget it. Not even a testicular tingle. Not one urge to get my dick wet. Not wanting to be a killjoy, I plastered a fake smile on my face. I fucking wasn't into it. In fact, I felt sick and wished I could take her by the haunches and shove her aside. Even pass her over to one of my stag mates. Out of the corner of my eye, I saw cameras on either side of the room. Damn. She could touch, but I couldn't. Physical contact wasn't allowed. I put my clammy palms under my ass so I wouldn't be tempted.

Seamlessly, a new song started up. Enrique Inglesias's "Baliando."

"I wanna be *contigo,*" purred my private dancer, in her cheap, nasal voice. To my utter horror, while she circled her soaked center around my cock, her Miley Cyrus length tongue trailed up my neck to my lips. While my pals howled like animals, I squirmed, forcing myself not to turn my head to avoid looking like a pussy. She might want to be with me, but I didn't want to be with her. Not one repulsive bit.

And then, I heard the hiss of a zipper. The sound of metal scraping against my dick. Shit. She was pulling down my fly. That did it. With a powerful thrust of my knees, and without touching her, I bounced her off my lap. Stunned, she fell onto one of the cylinder tables.

"What the fuck?" she hissed, collecting herself.

Not aware of what was really going on, shit-faced Jaime, Steve, and Jake applauded and blew wolf whistles.

"Give our boy a table dance," shouted Jaime, tucking a hundred dollar bill into her skimpy wet bottoms. He must have blown several thousand dollars at this pop stand.

I bolted to my feet.

"Where you going, dude?" asked Steve. "Need to wank off in the little boys room?"

I tried to keep my cool but was sweating like a pig.

I felt dirty and claustrophobic. Feigning fatigue once again and citing an early morning flight (which was at least true), I thanked my buds for my stag night.

"She's all yours, dudes." I didn't want to come across as a jackass.

"Man," said Jaime, his voice hoarse. "Are you wussing out on us?"

I missed my tiger. It was as simple as that.

I got back to the Bellagio at midnight. While I couldn't get the Presidential Suite reserved for high rollers, I had an almost as luxurious penthouse unit on the same floor. Wearily, I inserted my key card into the door, debating whether to call my tiger after taking a quick shower to rid myself of the stench of stale booze, smoke, and bad pussy. At this late hour, she could be sound asleep.

Except for the dazzling Vegas skyline shining through the floor to ceiling windows, the suite was pitch-black. I swear I'd left the lights on. Maybe the turndown service maid had turned them off. Whatever. I headed straight to my bedroom, ready to collapse into bed.

As I stepped into the dark room, a familiar voice sounded in my ears.

"Hi, Blake. Did you have fun?"

My nerves shorted out. I flipped on the light. "What the hell are you doing here?"

It was fucking Kat. Wearing nothing but a black lace push up bra and matching thong along with black patent stilettos. Perched on my bed with her knees bent and endless legs spread. She licked her lips.

"You could be a little happier to see me and say hello." She slid a hand beneath the lace bottoms.

My blood was sizzling. "How did you know I was here?"

"From your friend Jaime Zander. When I called him to discuss a bachelor party, he told me all about the one he had planned for you tonight."

"How did you get his number?" My voice was rising with anger.

She smiled smugly. "Daddy. Jaime handles all his advertising."

Mooreland Realty was one of the biggest realtors in the country. I had no idea Clayton Moore was one of Jaime's clients. That explained why Kat was at his art gallery opening last December.

"How did you get into my room?"

She batted her eyes. "It's amazing what a hundred dollar bill given to the right person can get you."

I'd give as many hundreds at it took to get her out of my room. And out of my life for good. It was time to cut to the chase.

"Kat, what the fuck do you want?"

"I want what we once had." She was fingering herself.

"We had nothing."

"We had Capri."

"It was just a summer fling. I ended it, but you have some kind of weird-ass obsession with me. You should be in therapy."

She let out a mocking laugh. "I've been in therapy my whole life. It's a joke."

Obviously, it was. She was still one sick chick.

She narrowed her eyes at me "You ruined it for me with all other men. No one fucks the way you do."

"I'm sure you can find someone," I said, wondering why the hell I was even having this conversation with her.

"We could have had it all, Blake. But you fucked it up."

"You fucked yourself." I spat out the words.

Anger washed over her face. Her eyes flared with fury. I was beginning to think she was bi-polar. I'd had enough.

"Please get the fuck out of here before I call security." I had to control myself from physically throwing her out the door.

Slowly and wordlessly, she made her way out of my bed. My eyes stayed fixed on her as she donned her pencil skirt and tight V-neck sweater. She grabbed her monstrous purse and marched to the door to my suite.

At the doorway, she turned and glared at me. A sinister smile curled on her lips.

"I'm going to prove how much *I* love you, Blake. I'm going to let *you* tell that classless, mousy fiancée of yours *all* about us."

I clenched my jaw and my fists. I'd never been this close to punching a woman. My blood pressure soaring, I held my breath and then let it go through my nose.

"Get the hell out of here, Kat. NOW!"

"Bye, Blakey," she retorted, her voice saccharine sweet. She turned on her heel and disappeared.

I sunk down on the couch and rubbed my temples. Tomorrow, when I got back to LA, I was going to have a heart-to-heart talk with my tiger. It was time she knew.

Chapter 17
Jennifer

Thank God, Blake was coming back tomorrow morning. The two weeks he'd been away felt like an eternity. And this last week had been pure misery.

I was bloated. Achy. Irritable. And tired. A total emotional wreck.

I cried at the littlest things. For no reason.

I yelled at sweet Mrs. Cho when she couldn't reach Blake.

I scribbled red-ink notes all over one of the scripts I was reading and couldn't focus on another.

I broke down and bawled in my support group when a new member shared her horrific story of being beaten and raped.

The pressures of work and the wedding were getting to me. And so was something else. I was over a week late for my period. *Stress?* Tossing the script I was reviewing, I googled my symptoms.

Oh shit!

If things couldn't get more complicated, an unexpected e-mail popped up in my inbox. The hair on the back of my neck bristled. It was from my ex-fiancé, Bradley Wick. I hadn't seen or heard from him since the time I ran into him and his fiancée Candace, registering at Bloomingdale's, and that was almost a year ago. I stared at my computer screen, my fingertips lightly drumming the keyboard. The only thing keeping me from deleting it was the subject line said URGENT in big shouty caps. With reservation, I opened it. The long and short of it—Bradley wanted to see me. He had something important he wanted to share. Despite my angst-out state, I agreed to meet him at lunch—at a nearby vegan restaurant. Some things never changed.

Mr. Punctuality was already seated at a table in the small, uncrowded restaurant. He'd already ordered one of those green soymilk concoctions he favored. Taking a seat across from him (yes, still the same ungentlemanly Bradley), I rested one hand on the table and the other, with Blake's ring, on my lap. I studied his face as he flashed that big toothy smile. The smile hadn't changed but his face had—he looked like he'd put on a fair amount of weight. He'd gotten jowly, and his receding hairline had receded further.

"Hi, Jennifer," he said, handing me a menu. "Thanks for coming."

"Sure, Bradley. No problem." Interestingly, I no longer felt anything toward him—neither rage nor contempt for having cheated on me with his hygienist. "You said it was urgent. Is something the matter?"

"I made a mistake."

I cocked my head. "What do you mean?"

"I should have married *you.*"

"Bradley, what are you talking about?"

"It didn't work out with Candace. She was a money grubbing wench. We just finalized our divorce. The bitch got the condo."

"I'm sorry to hear that." Okay. I had to admit it. My heart was doing a little jig. He'd gotten his comeuppance.

"I want us to get back together. Give it another chance." To my shock, he reached across the table and palmed my hand. I yanked it away.

"Bradley, I'm afraid that's not possible." My other hand flew up from under the table. I held it up, the glimmering snowflake diamond facing him. "I'm engaged."

Bradley's beady eyes darkened. "To who?"

"To my boss. Blake Burns."

Bradley's lips snarled. "To that fucking psychopath who practically bit off my fingers?"

I nodded. Bradley's face reddened with rage. He slammed his juice on the table.

"You're making the biggest mistake of your life."

"No, Bradley, the biggest mistake of my life would have been marrying you. Thank goodness, Blake sent me that video of you and Candace all over each other."

Bradley's eye grew wide with shock. "What! That

bastard shot that footage?"

Enough of this lunch; it was beginning to nauseate me. "Excuse me, Bradley. I'm going to use the restroom, and then I'm splitting."

Grabbing my shoulder bag, I stood up and then hurried to the restroom located in the back of the restaurant. Frequent urination. Another symptom. Fortunately, the small one-person unisex bathroom was vacant. I emptied my bladder, washed my hands, and unlocked the door. As I opened it, Bradley came charging in and pushed me backward until I was pinned against the wall. His newly flaccid body pressed against me and his small hands fondled my swollen breasts.

"Bradley, please let me go," I pleaded, trying to stay calm.

Madness flickered in his eyes. "No, not until you get another taste of me." He leaned into me with his mouth parted. His antiseptic breath skimmed my cheeks. To my horror, his repulsive lips were about to touch down on mine. *No fucking way.* Without over thinking, my knee came up and jabbed his groin. I heard him groan. *Bingo!* I'd gotten him right where I wanted. Right in the balls! The self-defense class Blake had made me take had paid off.

"Fuck!" he roared as he crumpled to the tiled floor. Clutching his crotch, he writhed in pain.

A victorious smile shimmered on my face, and then it fell off like a scab, giving way to cold fury. "Don't you ever contact me again, Dickwick. I'm so done with you."

He glared at me. "You're going to pay for this, Jennifer Fucking McCoy."

Without another word, I scurried out of the restroom, my stomach cramping.

On the way back to the office, I made a stop. At a CVS drugstore. There was something I needed to buy. There was something I needed to know.

And soon enough I did.

Chapter 18
Blake

I got on an early morning flight and was back in LA by seven a.m. I had my driver take me straight to my apartment. I couldn't wait to see my tiger. I was going to fuck her senseless, and then I was going to tell her. The sour taste of Kat was still in my mouth. I had to cleanse myself of her. I'd buried the truth six feet under, but now I had to expose it before it blew up in my face. My stomach knotted as I inserted the key into the door lock. A cocktail of guilt and anxiety coursed through my blood. I hadn't rehearsed any kind of confession, nor did I have any idea how she would react to what I was about to tell her. I'd made a stupid, stupid mistake.

Expecting to see my early riser in the kitchen making coffee, I was surprised when she wasn't there. Dropping my bag, I padded to our bedroom. With the blackout curtains drawn, the room was dark. I could hear her soft breaths. Quietly, I traipsed over to the bed. She was still sound asleep, a script by her side. She looked so beautiful and peaceful. Despite my physical and emotional needs, I couldn't wake her. I headed to the bathroom to wash up and then I shed my clothes and crawled bone naked into the bed. Before I could get under the covers, she stirred.

"Blake?" she said sleepily. Her eyes fluttered open and she twitched a small smile.

"Baby, what are you still doing in bed? I thought you'd be getting ready for work."

She groaned. I smoothed her hair. "Are you okay?

"I got my period. It's super heavy and I have really bad cramps." She grimaced. "I'm almost two weeks late."

My stomach twisted. While she was still on the pill, I hadn't used a condom in almost a year. The chances were slim but still possible.

"Do you think you had a miscarriage?" Saying that last word pained me.

She shook her head. "No. I took a pregnancy test yesterday. It was negative."

I felt partly relieved, but worry still gnawed at me.

She sat up slowly. The pinched expression on her face told me she was in pain. She held a hand to her belly.

"I'm going to head into the office a little later if that's okay with you."

"No, it's not okay. I want you to stay home and rest."

"But Blake, I've got so much to do. And with the

wedding and everything—"

"Fuck it. It'll all get done. And I want you to see my sister. She's the best gynecologist in town."

I held her in my arms. "I've missed you, baby."

"The same," she said softly as I planted a kiss on her scalp.

Fucking my tiger wasn't happening. And the dreaded conversation I wanted to have with her would have to wait.

Chapter 19
Jennifer

"Hi, Marcy. Thanks for seeing me on such short notice." I'd actually had to wait almost two weeks for my lunchtime appointment—until my much longer than usual period subsided. I'd been so looking forward to accompanying Blake at lunch to pick out a new tux for the wedding, but he was insistent on me seeing his sister at the very first opportunity. Health came first.

"Not a problem, Jennifer. Fortunately, I had a cancellation." Her voice was professional but warm. Clad in a stylish slacks outfit under her lab coat, she looked a little trimmer since I'd last seen her, and she was wearing more makeup. She actually looked very pretty.

She continued. "What brings you here?"

Sitting with one leg folded over the other on an examining room table, I told her that I hadn't been to a gynecologist since grad school, and that I was experiencing some cramping and heavy bleeding with my period. It had lasted ten days.

"Are you on the pill?" she asked.

"Yes." I nodded.

"Okay, what I'd like you to do is to undress and put on the robe, leaving it open in the front. I'll be right back." She ambled out of the small room, closing the door behind her.

I eyed the blue paper robe sitting next to me on the table. In no time, I was undressed and wearing the flimsy contraption. Still seated on the table, I surveyed my surroundings. Unlike the campus doctor's examination room, it was full of personality. Marcy's numerous degrees and awards took up space on the walls along with many charming framed pieces of artwork done by her children. One, a painting of SpongeBob, brightened my spirits.

Blake's sister returned in no time. She shot me a small smile. I think this was a first.

"Jennifer, I'd like you to lie down."

Doing as she asked with my knees steepled, I watched as she slid out two metal stirrups from the examining table.

"Now slide your rear down to the edge and put your feet in these."

Familiar with this routine, I did as she asked. The jolt of cold metal against the heels of my bare feet sent a shiver up my spine.

"Perfect." Facing me, she inserted a gloved hand into my center, gently pressing and moving around it. She closed her eyes while doing the pelvic exam.

"You're very tiny," she commented.

"Yeah, I know," I replied, hoping she wasn't going to say something like: "How does my brother get his huge cock inside you?" Or: "Does it hurt when he fucks you?" The truth: Blake fit inside me beautifully, and it felt fucking great.

As Marcy probed with her gloved fingers, I suddenly imagined Blake here doing the same. Feeling me up and then fucking me wildly with my feet anchored in these stirrups. He'd once told me he'd done that to a high school teacher and had gotten caught by his sister. Such a bad boy. A sudden distraught thought made me shudder: Had he ever done that to Kat?

"Are you okay?" asked Marcy, obviously feeling me squirm.

"Yes, everything's good." I forced Kat to the back of my head. Whatever she had with Blake was ancient history. I shouldn't care. Yet, I did.

Marcy continued to probe.

"Did you find anything?" My voice was peppered with concern. She seemed to be spending an unusually long time exploring my privates.

She opened her eyes and removed her hand. "So far, everything seems normal."

Relieved, I kept my eyes on her as she reached for the speculum on the mobile tray table beside her. I hated this part of the exam.

"Now, I'm going to insert this into your vagina and

then do a pap smear. "Let me know if it hurts," she said as she adjusted the metal clamp between my legs.

While it was definitely uncomfortable, it didn't hurt. Marcy had a very gentle touch. My eyes stayed on her as she swabbed me twice, once with a small spatula and then again with a small bristle brush. She dipped each into separate vials that were filled with liquid and labeled with my name.

"Are we done?" I asked, eager to leave.

"I'd like to do one more thing. An ultrasound just to do a double check."

I'd never had one before. "Isn't that what they do for pregnant women?" I shivered. Maybe I was pregnant and that stupid store-bought test was wrong.

"Yes," she said, first pressing down on my abdomen. "Does this hurt?"

I had to be honest. "Just a little."

Her lips pinched, she pressed down harder. I gave a little yelp. A frisson of fear rippled through me. "Is that normal?"

"Yes. Some women are just very sensitive. If you really had a lot of pain, you would have jumped off the table."

Inwardly, I sighed with relief as Marcy wheeled the ultra-sound machine closer to me. It consisted of a monitor and some kind of computer with lots of buttons and attachments. She then lifted up my paper gown and rubbed some gel on my tummy. The surprising warmth of it contrasted sharply with the chill of the air conditioning.

"Is this going to hurt?" I asked, fear creeping into my voice.

"Not at all." She smiled again. "It may even tickle."

I watched as she glided the head of a shaver-shaped probe around my belly while her other hand fiddled with the buttons and keys on the computer. She was right. It did tickle.

Her intense blue eyes alternated between my abdomen and the screen as did mine. I was intrigued by the volcano-like image on the screen, but had no clue what it was.

"Hmm," she murmured, her eyes on the monitor.

My muscles tensed. "Is something wrong with me?"

"You have a number of fibroid tumors on your uterus." She pointed them out to me on the monitor. They looked like shadowy dark spots. There were five in total.

"Oh my God. Are they dangerous?" Panic shot through me. *Tumors?* The C-word was on the tip of my tongue.

"Actually, they're very common and benign. Many women have them although they're a little unusual for someone as young as you. They explain your heavy, irregular period and the cramping."

"What should I do?" I asked anxiously as she cleaned off my shiny tummy with one of those moist wipes.

"Really nothing. We'll just have to monitor them to watch how fast they grow and see if they affect your ability to get pregnant."

My panic button sounded. I was such an alarmist. "Does that mean I won't be able to have a baby?"

"Not at all. Most of the time, they're harmless and very slow growing. If they do interfere with your ability to conceive, they can be laparoscopically removed."

"Laparoscopically?" I could barely pronounce the scary-sounding word.

"It's a noninvasive surgical procedure. It's rather painless and can be done as an out-patient." She set the probe down on the ultrasound stand while I lay there motionless. Worry was etched on my face.

"Jennifer, honestly, there's no need to worry at this point," Marcy said with a comforting smile. "I want you to stay on the pill and eat foods rich with iron so you don't get anemic. Just let me know if you experience any unusual discomfort." She took off her latex gloves and washed her hands as I collected myself.

"Would you like to have lunch?" she asked. "I close the office and take an hour break every day. There's a great little coffee shop downstairs."

I was pleasantly surprised by her offer. I'd never spent a lot of time with Blake's sister. And Blake rarely socialized with her. Maybe this would be a good opportunity to get to know her and learn more about their brother-sister relationship. And she was, after all, going to be one of my bridesmaids.

The coffee shop Marcy took me to was right next door to her office. It was small and totally unpretentious and kind of reminded me of the old fashioned coffee shops in Boise. We both ordered iron-rich medium rare burgers and kale salads, along with Cokes—she, a diet one and I, a cherry one.

I anxiously bit into my delicious burger, not quite knowing what to say to her. Marcy, on the other hand, wasted no time starting a conversation.

"I thought we should get to know each other since we're going to be sisters-in-law."

Swallowing, I agreed. "Thanks for inviting for me for lunch."

"My pleasure." She took a sip of her soda through her straw. "You're probably wondering why Blake and I don't get along that well."

Ten years younger than Marcy, he had mentioned once that the two of them fought all the time as children. "He doesn't really talk about it much," I replied. "Mostly, he refers to you as being the best gynecologist in all of LA." *The truth.*

Marcy's eyes widened with surprise. "He said something nice about me?"

"Yes. He's very proud of you."

With that, Marcy began to tell me what it was like growing up with Blake. She had enjoyed being an only child, and though never the beauty her mother was, her parents lavished her with attention. She was quite the bookworm and pleaser, always studying and scoring high grades. She sounded a lot like me.

When Blake came along, everything changed. The beautiful blue-eyed baby was the apple of everyone's eyes. The center of attention. No matter how mischievous he was, he got away with everything. Marcy grew jealous of Blake, who knew how to wrap both his father and mother around his little finger. And his grandma too. While sixteen-year-old Marcy was going through an awkward stage with raging hormones and pimples, six-year-old Blake was getting more adorable each day.

"I felt threatened by him," Marcy sighed. "I was the smart one, but I really wanted to be the beautiful one." She paused to sip her Coke. "Thank goodness, I have identical twins. And even if they weren't, I'd never pit one against the other that way. Or lavish more attention on one over the other."

I processed what she'd said. Being an only child, I had no clue about sibling rivalry. I stored her information in my mind for the future.

"How are Jonathan and Jackson doing?" I interjected.

"Thanks for asking. They're actually doing surprisingly well. In fact, better now that Matt and I are separated. I think all our fighting really affected them. Kids model themselves after their parents' behaviors."

More words of wisdom. And so true. I was so much like my pleasing mother, so non-confrontational. And I dissected things like my father. I told Marcy I was sorry about her marriage.

"Don't be. We weren't good for each other. It was a marriage of rebellion and convenience—he was a good-looking poor guy and I came from a lot of money. But we didn't make the other half better."

I thought hard about what Marcy had just said. Blake was still cocky, stuck-up, and arrogant. Maybe we weren't meant . . .

Before I could finish my thought, Marcy jumped in. "Jennifer, I just want to tell you that you are so good for Blake. You make him better. I see the way he acts around you. He's sweet, considerate, and loving. He's more patient and so much less into himself."

"But he's still so cocky and self-assured."

Marcy rolled her eyes. "You have no idea. And those bimbos he used to hang with . . ."

"Do you know Kat Moore?" The question slipped out of my mouth.

Marcy's blue eyes darkened. "That girl is pure trouble. Stay away from her."

"She's helping plan our wedding."

"Be careful. Don't let her manipulate you." She

pressed her lips thin as if she wanted to tell me more and was holding back words. Before I could ask her what she meant, she changed the subject.

"The boys are so excited about being the ring bearers. But they've been fighting over who's carrying which ring."

Still mulling her previous words, I feigned a chuckle. The check came and Marcy reached for it. Her treat. She smiled warmly at me and then did something unexpected—she affectionately clasped my hands in hers.

"Jennifer, I'm so glad you're marrying Blake. You're the best thing that's ever happened to him. I'm thrilled you're going to be my sister-in-law."

We ended lunch with a hug. A new mission impossible awaited me. I was determined to get Blake to like his sister as much as I did.

Chapter 20

Blake

I owned half a dozen tuxes, but Jennifer was insistent I get a brand new one for our wedding. One that had never been photographed at the many galas I'd attended or touched by one of my former hook-ups.

Driving my Porsche with the top down, I headed to Beverly Hills where I was going to meet with my personal shopper, Daniel, at the Saks Fifth Avenue Men's Store. I was actually looking forward to it. Unlike a lot of men who hated shopping for clothes, I actually loved it. And I especially loved buying beautiful Italian designer suits. I must have owned over two hundred of them. Jennifer's analytical friend Libby called me a metrosexual, and one night when we went out for dinner, she made me take a *Cosmopolitan* magazine quiz.

1. You just can't walk past a beauty supply store without making a purchase. *True.*

2. You own fifty pairs of shoes, a dozen pairs of sunglasses, just as many watches and you only wear

Calvin Klein briefs. *True*.

3. Mani-pedi is part of your vocabulary. *True*.

4. You shave more than just your face. You also exfoliate and moisturize. *True*.

5. You can't imagine a day without hair styling products. *True*.

6. You spend more time in the bathroom showering and grooming than your girlfriend. *True*.

7. You carry a man bag. *False*.

Okay, so, I blew one question (guess which one), but I was a high maintenance kind of guy. Trust me, any rich, good-looking guy who tells you he isn't is full of shit. Jennifer couldn't believe I had to annex my closet to make extra room for all my suits—and all my grooming products. She'd threatened to buy me a man bag for Christmas. But that's where I drew the line. No fucking way. Our silly squabble flashed into my mind as I valeted my car at the back entrance of the venerable department store. As competent as I was when it came to suiting myself up, I wished she were here with me. But I didn't want her to miss her hard-to-get appointment with my sister, and she didn't want me to postpone the fitting with the wedding so close. It was less than a month away.

The valet attendant welcomed me warmly as I stepped out of the car. I was a familiar face. While a lot of guys I knew, including Jaime Zander, preferred to shop at hip Barney's down the street, I liked Saks. Because all three floors of the store catered only to men, it was kind of a refuge. The last place I'd get assaulted by a blond bimbo. Besides, this is where my father shopped and his father before him. Legacy.

Upon entering the store, I headed to the elevator and took it straight to the third floor. Daniel met me quickly. To my astonishment, I was the sole customer. Well, at least I'd get done quickly. In fact, I knew what tux I liked already—it was draped on a mannequin. Simple. Elegant. A one-buttoned tapered jacket and a thin satin stripe along the pants leg. The kind Brad Pitt might wear.

"An excellent choice," commented the perfectly groomed, androgynous Daniel. "An Armani. It just came in. I'll retrieve one in your size and send Luigi to the dressing room to tailor it."

Five minutes later, I was looking, if I have say to so myself, damn good in my new tux, complete with a slick new tux shirt and bow tie as well as a snappy pocket square in my signature blue. The spacious dressing room was the size of a guest room, done up in soothing shades of gray. Standing before the tri-fold mirror, I watched as Luigi, my tailor, expertly made some alterations. A stocky Italian craftsman in his late seventies with a shock of never-graying jet black hair, he'd been with the store forever and had tailored both my father's and grandfather's suits. He was practically family.

"*Howsa* your grandma?" he asked in his still thick Italian accent as he squatted down and let out the hem of the pants to accommodate my long legs.

"She's great." I'd long suspected that Luigi had a crush on Grandma.

"You tell her Luigi give her his love." I made a mental note: Invite Luigi to the wedding. Grandma needed a date. *And* sex.

Luigi stuck a few pins along the legs of the pants, taking them in. I always took one size bigger because I needed the extra crotch room. While the crotch could be let out, having pins anywhere near my dick gave me testicular tingles—not the good kind.

"So *who'sa* the lucky girl?"

"Her name is Jennifer. You'll meet her, Luigi, at the next fitting."

"Luigi cannot wait." He finished up. "*All-a* done." The jovial Italian reassembled his tailoring kit. He carefully helped me off with the jacket and then left me alone in the dressing room, closing the door behind him.

About to unbutton the pinned-up trousers, I heard a knock on the door. I recognized the voice. Daniel.

"Mr. Burns, your fiancée is here. May I send her back?"

"Of course." That was just like my tiger to surprise me. A rush of tingles spread from my head to my toes.

The thought of having a little quicky with her right here in this dressing room sent my dick into a dither. I could feel it rise and harden against the fine wool fabric of my trousers. Maybe I'd wall-bang her or fuck her over the velvet bench or have a roll on the carpet. We could even watch ourselves come in the tri-fold mirror. My pulse quickened as the unlocked door swung open.

"Hi, Blake."

My jaw dropped to the floor and so did my cock.

I watched in the mirror as one of her long, toned bare arms wrapped around my shoulder while the other one grabbed my crotch. Hot kisses singed the back of my neck. Every muscle in my body clenched.

"Kat, what the fuck are you doing here?" Rage fueled every word, but I didn't move, afraid her claws would dig into my balls.

"You know you want me." Smirking, she squeezed my equipment harder. I yelped. And then, in one swift move, she unbuttoned the tuxedo pants and unzipped the fly. The pants slid down to my feet. She worked her hand under my briefs.

"Fucking let go of me." Impulsively, I jerked myself free, almost smashing into the mirror.

I turned to face her. "Get the hell out of here."

Her fierce green eyes pierced me like poisonous darts. "You should be marrying me, Blake, not that pathetic excuse for a woman. You need a Rolls Royce, not a pickup truck."

"Don't you ever fucking talk about my future wife like that." Seething mad, I clutched the tails of my tux shirt so I wouldn't raise a hand and slap the shit out of her.

Another smirk flashed on her face and then she huffed. "Are you threatening me, Blake?"

I didn't respond. "Just. Go."

"Does Jennifer know yet what *really* happened?"

My blood curdled. I still hadn't told her. I sucked in a gulp of the thickening air. "We don't sit around talking about you. We're too busy fucking like bunnies."

"Ha! Aren't you the funny one? Well, you're fucking with the wrong person."

Her double entendre wasn't lost on me. "You mind your own damn business, Kat, and keep your fucking mouth shut. And if you come near me one more time, I'm going to get a restraining order."

Collecting herself, she smirked yet again. "Oh, is that another threat? Don't worry, Blake."

With a fling of her mane of hair, she slithered out the door.

Chapter 21
Jennifer

I wove down trafficky Santa Monica Boulevard enroute to my office. Adele's "Rumor Has It" was playing on the radio.

My mind occupied, I forced myself to pay attention to the congested road. The findings of Marcy's examination were unsettling. While she seemed nonplussed, I was concerned. A new F-bomb. Fibroids. As I sat at what felt like forever at a red light, I debated whether or not I should tell Blake about them. With the wedding getting closer, we just didn't need more stress.

And while our lunch had drawn us closer, one of his sister's remarks had made my blood bubble. Yes, it didn't take a rocket scientist to figure out Kat was trouble . . . but what did she mean about not letting her manipulate me? The way she immediately switched the subject made me think there was something more. Something she wasn't telling me.

My mind drifted to Blake, and I glanced at my dashboard clock. It was almost one thirty. I wondered—was he still at his tux fitting? Maybe there was still time to show up and surprise him. Saks was only one turn away. Using my Bluetooth, I speed-dialed him. It went straight to his answering machine. I bypassed leaving a message. When the light turned green, I decided to take a chance. I made a sharp right onto Beverly Drive and headed south toward Wilshire.

My cell phone rang. A familiar number. I hit answer. My heart leapt into my throat.

Horns blared at me as I ran a red light.

Oh. My. God. *No!*

The End of THAT MAN 4

THAT MAN 5

The gripping, epic conclusion to the THAT MAN wedding story.

Be prepared to laugh, cry, and swoon!

COMING DECEMBER 2014

ACKNOWLEDGMENTS

I'm going to keep this short and sweet as I will be writing a book-length list of all those I want to thank for sharing this rollercoaster ride at the end of THAT MAN 5. Big shout-outs go to the following:

My wonderfully honest and insightful Beta readers. In alphabetical order: Kelly Butterfield, Amber Escalera, Kellie Fox, Kashunna Fly, Gloria Herrera, Wanda Kather, Adriane Leigh, Cindy Meyer, Jenn Moshe, Arianne Richmonde, and Karen Moshe Silverstein.

My terrific family for putting up with me (and boy, have they!).

All the hardworking bloggers who have supported and embraced THAT MAN.

And finally, never last nor least, my incredible readers. You are the reason I write.

I love you all!

♥ MWAH!

ABOUT THE AUTHOR

Nelle L'Amour is a *New York Times* and *USA Today* bestselling author who lives in Los Angeles with her Prince Charming-ish husband, twin teenage princesses, and a bevy of royal pain-in-the-butt pets. A former executive in the entertainment and toy industries with a prestigious Humanitus Award to her credit, she gave up playing with Barbies a long time ago but still enjoys playing with toys with her husband. While she writes in her PJs, she loves to get dressed up and pretend she's Hollywood royalty.

Her books include the highly rated *Seduced by the Park Avenue Billionaire Boxed Set, Undying Love, Gloria's Secret*, *Gloria's Revenge* and the *That Man* series. *Gloria's Forever*, a novella, will be published in early 2015.

Nelle loves to hear from her readers.

Sign up for her newsletter: http://eepurl.com/N3AXb

Email her at: nellelamour@gmail.com

Like her on Facebook: facebook.com/NelleLamourAuthor

And connect to her on Twitter: twitter.com/nellelamour

Printed in Germany
by Amazon Distribution
GmbH, Leipzig